A Candlelight Ecstasy Romance ®

"WE DON'T LIVE OUR LIVES THE SAME WAY," SIMON WAS SAYING.
"OR LIKE THE SAME THINGS. IT JUST WOULDN'T WORK."

Nodding agreement that she suddenly didn't feel, Joanna wondered who needed more convincing. "You're right, Simon. I mean, my God, you take everything so seriously. I suppose I'm rather casual."

"You're a junk-food junkie—*and* a nibbler," he accused lightly. "I, on the other hand, like balanced meals. Three times a day."

"Of course, and you—you wash as you go along," she said. "I can't face the kitchen without a nap first."

"Yes, and you sleep late. I get up early."

"I'm tolerant. You're not. You're rather stuffy. I'm not," Joanna countered.

"Don't start with me, Joanna. Let's at least be civil."

CANDLELIGHT ECSTASY ROMANCES®

STAND STILL
THE MOMENT

Margaret Dobson

A CANDLELIGHT ECSTASY ROMANCE®

Published by
Dell Publishing Co., Inc.
1 Dag Hammarskjold Plaza
New York, New York 10017

Dell ® TM 681510, Dell Publishing Co., Inc.

Candlelight Ecstasy Romance®, 1,203,540, is a registered
trademark of Dell Publishing Co., Inc., New York, New York.

ISBN: 0-440-18197-6

Printed in the United States of America
First printing—January 1985

To him who vows he cannot stay forever,
But won't deny the momentary thrill,
Beware the one whose whisper leaves you breathless.
Her heart commands the moment to stand still.

Granny

To Our Readers:

We have been delighted with your enthusiastic response to Candlelight Ecstasy Romances®, and we thank you for the interest you have shown in this exciting series.

In the upcoming months we will continue to present the distinctive, sensuous love stories you have come to expect only from Ecstasy. We look forward to bringing you many more books from your favorite authors and also the very finest work from new authors of contemporary romantic fiction.

As always, we are striving to present the unique, absorbing love stories that you enjoy most—books that are more than ordinary romance.

Your suggestions and comments are always welcome. Please write to us at the address below.

Sincerely,

The Editors
Candlelight Romances
1 Dag Hammarskjold Plaza
New York, New York 10017

CHAPTER ONE

The day lilies were finally blooming. After years of trying new mulches and scowling over failures, he had finally coaxed the bulbs to produce aromatic yellow flowers, which lined the narrow stone walkway to his door.

Satisfied, Simon smiled. He'd never been a great gardener, but now and then his efforts panned out. And he could admit, to himself, that victory was a tad sweeter knowing that Susan—who had seen herself as an excellent gardener—had had no luck at all with lilies. Too bad his ex-wife wasn't here now to admit that his hands were *not* too big for *sensitive* gardening, as she had so righteously termed it.

Simon drew the ivory-sheer curtains farther apart to take in the pleasant scene of late summer in a small community just outside Springfield. A few silver maples splashed flamboyant color farther down the street, following the curve of the cul-de-sac. But he preferred the stately pin oaks that stood as natural sentries for the

11

conservative red-brick arches of his older two-story home.

It was an orderly, quiet neighborhood. Perfect, to his way of thinking. Simon's lips curved in appreciation as he tried not to let pestering thoughts intrude.

But they did nonetheless.

He didn't want a woman in his house. For many reasons. Male tenants were easier to get along with. He had hardly ever seen Richard. He'd never even thought about Richard unless he'd wanted to. But a woman . . . well, it changed things. Simon didn't know exactly how, but it damned sure changed things. You couldn't ignore women. They didn't allow it. A woman wouldn't go about her business and leave him alone. She would involve him in her life in some way. She would want to be nice and have dinner together once a week at least. Go places together. Send him a card on his birthday and expect one in return.

Yet, here he was, waiting for Joanna Sinclair. And he didn't much like waiting. She might be a nationally known spitfire of a consumer advocate, come to bestow her wisdom on Houghton College. But obviously the consumption of time—his time, anyway—meant little to her. Despite misgivings about having her also take Richard's apartment, Simon had decided to play the polite host and at least introduce the woman to her side of the house. But if she didn't arrive soon she would have to show herself in. He was due at the college in half an hour.

There was nothing too distracting about the white El Camino that zipped onto his street from the main avenue. That wouldn't be her, Simon thought, imagining Joanna Sinclair as more of a low-slung sporty type. In

12

any case, no sister of Richard Sinclair would tool around in a truck. The driver was probably lost, as often happened in this neighborhood.

Satisfied when the truck had negotiated the wide curve of the cul-de-sac and was headed toward the avenue again, Simon started to turn away. But the sudden revving of a motor recaptured his attention. He remained at the window, his square chin lifting in wary alert.

His green gaze narrowed as the El Camino lurched to a halt at the curb in front of his house. It was then that he noticed all the . . . things in the back of the truck. A metal door slammed smartly and his hand slid downward, along the smooth grain of the drapery until he unknowingly clenched the material.

My God. It *was* Joanna Sinclair. He sensed it with all the caution in his bones.

One tawny brow lifted as he watched the woman come around to lower a squeaky tailgate and lever herself easily onto the truck bed. She was smaller, more fragile-looking than he had expected. After hearing Richard recite her long list of accomplishments, Simon had imagined an Amazon at the very least. She was a "champion of the people," after all. Who could fault him for assuming she'd have some muscle to go with her crusading image?

She was shifting her belongings to the edge of the truck bed. A leather valise dropped with a thump. A bushel basket of odds and ends came next, and then—two shiny aluminum trash cans. The irritating scrape of heavy metal grated along his spine. Damn, she was noisy. And she'd brought her own cans. He'd gladly supplied Richard with cans. *What* was she doing? He ought to go out and inform her that her entrance was around back through the alley, he supposed.

But Simon didn't. Instead, he watched her pause, temporarily quiet and looking much like a peacock as she placed small fists on trim hips and turned in a circular survey of her surroundings. From front to back a navy-blue tee shirt hugged her feminine curves. A polka-dot bow brought thick, dark hair under control at the nape of a slender neck. Wearing snug-fitting jeans and summer sandals, she didn't appear much the athletic type. Thank God for that. But she did look healthy and . . . spunky.

He hated spunky.

It was such a frustrating trait. And when he saw the slow, dissatisfied shake of her head as though offering smug comment on the neighborhood, his neighborhood, his preconception of her lowered another notch. Why that snob. What did she want? A high-rise apartment house with people stacked on top of each other?

Simon swallowed. He wasn't going to like this. He just knew it. But he had agreed to it. Joanna Sinclair would take over her brother's apartment and his classes at the college for the fall semester. Now there was nothing to do but steel himself to sharing his kitchen with a spunky—he groaned inside—stranger. A female stranger. And that, after all, was the crux of the matter.

And how was she going to view this one semester of teaching? Would she look at it as merely a favor to her brother? Something to get through so that she could return to the easy life of the lecture circuit? Or would he, as chairman of the economics department, have to cope with uncontrollable enthusiasm, as so often happened with novice teachers who aimed to set the world on fire before Christmas break?

Any of the above would be irritating, Simon surmised as she sprinted over to the side of the truck and reached up to capture one can in a bear hug. The can, its dome lid secured by some kind of strap, was lowered slowly to the grass, only to be turned onto its side—what was she doing? Richard had said she was a bit unconventional. Simon now thought that appraisal overgenerous. A middle-of-the-road person like himself would be asking too much, he supposed, his head tilting in mild wonder at the rather dainty foot poised atop the can . . . a can that was now rolling over his day lilies.

He stiffened. What the *hell* was she doing? The hot question tightened his jaw as he strode to the hallway and took firm hold of the doorknob. He would damned sure find out.

Correcting the direction of her cargo with another shove of her foot, Joanna backtracked to begin placing more of her belongings on the grass. God, what a pristine place, she mused. The geometric design of the shrubbery was enough to make her hightail it right back to Tulsa. No wonder Richard had left town before she arrived. He knew this wasn't her style, manicured lawns and privacy fences.

The basket containing bed linens and a reading lamp went next to her overnight case. Richard had seemed happy enough leasing one side of this huge old house. But she wasn't Richard. Come to think of it, she and her brother had never shared the same tastes, Joanna conceded with a small smile. Richard—in his endearing way—was a bit of a fuddy-duddy. A place for everything and everything in its place. In any case, she was to share only a kitchen with Gregory. She hardly ever gave kitchens a second thought. And if he was the kind who got testy over nail holes, well . . . she could handle that. For a while. Now if she could only get out of this heat . . .

Slamming the tailgate, Joanna stood tall. Hands on hips, she thrust out her chest and bent backward, allowing stiff muscles a good stretch.

"Dr. Sinclair, do you—"

Simon was startled at first by the sudden protuberance of her breasts. But he guessed his reaction was nothing compared to the becoming patches of warmth on her cheeks or the surprise in the wide blue eyes she turned up to him. There was the slightest pinch at one corner of a generous mouth. Both her face and her chest recovered quickly though.

Stepping onto the curb, she smiled and held out a hand. "Hi, there. You must be Simon Gregory. Richard's had such good things to say about you."

Simon let out a slow breath. Oh, she was smooth, this one. But he was undaunted. After all, the overturned can was right beside him as evidence. With a curt nod, he took her hand briefly and let it go again. "Do you have something against horticulture?"

Acutely aware of the edge in his deep voice, Joanna stared curiously for a moment, lowering her hand slowly to pick at the flat-fell seam of her jeans. He was younger than she had imagined. Rather nice-looking . . . in a stern sort of way. Thirty-six. Thirty-seven at the outside. But she didn't know what the hell he was talking about. And so she shrugged. "Not especially—"

"And yet you seem bent on destroying my efforts."

A hell of a welcome, Joanna decided, but she could

16

overlook that . . . for now. His cool gaze appeared to be focused just to the left of her sandals. She looked down, too, and saw the rather ugly flowers. Surely he wasn't upset by a few grazed petals. One stem might be bent, but certainly not broken.

"These?" she asked with amusement. "Why you couldn't *blast* these out of the ground. They grow like weeds in my backyard at home."

He didn't seem at all reassured. "What kind of mulch do you use?" he asked suspiciously.

"Mulch?" Oh, God. A mulcher. Joanna checked a cheeky smile. She cared nothing for day lilies and mowed hers down every chance she got. "Oh, I use whatever's handy to take care of my lilies." A Lawnboy mower works quite well, she added silently.

"I bet you don't roll garbage cans over them. Look, Doctor, you can see that in this neighborhood, we take pride in our lawns—"

"Yes, I can see that," she admitted, resigned to that fact. "And I apologize for any damages. Now, why don't you call me Joanna? We're going to be neighbors, you know."

"Yes—I know." There was a maddening tinge of regret in his tone as he crossed tanned forearms to rest on what surely must be a muscular chest beneath that crisp, white shirt. "As I was saying, it's a nice, quiet street and . . ."

"Um," she agreed absently. "Dead ends usually are."

Again she felt green eyes narrow in her direction. Joanna thought he would have very nice eyes if he would stop regarding her with such coolness.

"Around here it's called a cul-de-sac." He smiled—through a set of full, if rather tight, lips.

17

"Ah." She returned the smile in kind. "Well, I believe in calling a spade a spade." And a snob, a snob. Boy, did she want to roll her eyes right now. Instead she rolled the can another few feet.

"Why are you doing that?"

"Because it's easier than carrying it," she replied. Aware that he dogged her steps, Joanna gave the heavy aluminum cylinder another shove.

"There are better ways to move your can," Simon stated.

Somehow she had known there would be. Becoming impatient, Joanna turned back to him, cocking her head in an irresistible tease. "You know, you're right. I should've backed my truck right up to the porch."

To his credit, Simon Gregory's eyes didn't widen at the thought of tire tracks on his lawn. In fact he appeared quite calm as he said, "That isn't what I meant." But his chiseled lips hardly moved when he said it. "The alley at the rear of the house would have been much more convenient."

"Oh." It was a moot point since most of her things were already in a heap on the ground. "I'll move it later," she said, trying to maintain a slowly fading good humor. "First, I'll take what I have here inside. Do you think the rest of my things will still be on the truck when I come back?"

"Of course," he said in a droll tone. "I hear the El Camino Bandito is working the other side of town today."

After a slight pause of surprise, Joanna's smile came sincerely this time. Feeling somehow lighter, cooler, she allowed herself a tinkle of a chuckle. Simon's expression, however, remained unchanged, refusing to acknowledge that she found him amusing. The Ice Man definitely cometh, she thought with a sigh. Still, there was slightly less edge to his voice when he spoke again.

"I have a few minutes before I have to leave. I'll help."

"Why, thank you."

Reaching for the handle, Simon set the can upright, nursing a frown and a new respect for her strength as he did so. "What's in here? Bricks?"

Joanna shrugged. "Books. And a few small appliances."

As she hoisted her share of the weight and walked, garbage can between herself and Dr. Gregory, Joanna found graceful strides out of the question. She felt very much like C3PO toddling along arm in arm with R2D2. And come to think of it, Simon Gregory did favor the attractive Han Solo around the eyes—a slightly older, more somber Han Solo, admittedly, but with the same air of confidence. However, Joanna sensed that Simon's disposition fit Darth Vader more than any other character in the *Star Wars* saga.

Making her way up the sidewalk, she unconsciously aimed her feet toward the wide front door. Just before they reached the steps, Simon pulled both woman and can to the left for the trek to the side of the house.

"Your door is this way."

"It isn't necessary to jerk," she suggested calmly.

"It wasn't a jerk," he said with equal calm. "I merely applied the pressure needed to get the job done. By the way, I hope you won't make a habit of parking out front. I wouldn't want a path worn across this part of the lawn."

"Right." What did he think she was—a herd of buffalo? This man was going to have to loosen up a lot before *she* could get along with him.

When they reached the entrance that was obviously *hers*, Simon negotiated the two steps, pushed open the door and, with a modified sweep of his free hand, invited her to enter before him. Leading the ungainly trio single-file across the threshold, Joanna banged the can smartly against the doorjamb. The subsequent ricochet to the opposite side made her wince, but she didn't turn around.

"Uh . . . care to conga?" she asked in an effort to take his mind off what she sensed would be a search for sharp nicks in the wood.

The voice behind her was almost as cool as the air-conditioned room. "How about a highland fling?"

Her brows lifted in caution. "That depends on whom you have in mind to fling."

"This can, if you don't hurry up and tell me where you want it. I'd like to see if my fingers are still attached to my hand."

Joanna knew that feeling. "Right here will do for now." Carefully, she set the cargo down near the oval dining table and began to flex her own stiff fingers. A brief glimpse of the spacious living/dining room was all she got before Joanna sensed her helper's impatience to get on with the job at hand. He was already stepping outside again.

"Nice," she commented tentatively, her image of high ceilings and classically styled cornice work fading as she followed him into the sunshine. Watching his long masculine strides, Joanna allowed herself private enjoyment of the view. The outline of sinewy muscles pressing boldly against his trouser legs as he bent to

20

pick up a piece of her luggage commanded her full attention. *"Very* nice," she whispered and meant it sincerely this time. But was he always this stiff? This brusque?

After the second trash can was placed inside the apartment, they worked separately, passing each other with awkward nods of recognition on the path from curb to door. Simon said very little, for the most part avoiding her gaze. But each time she met him, Joanna added more information to her growing catalogue of masculine characteristics.

He had good hands. Strong and sure, judging by the confident way he took charge of her belongings. They might be gentle too, but Joanna saw no good reason to dwell on that question. There was no gold band either, in keeping with his divorced state. She knew about that. Richard had moved in a few months after the former Mrs. Simon Gregory had left the premises the year before. But that didn't necessarily mean anything. Some men mentally continued to be married long after they had signed the divorce papers. Was Simon one of those? Something certainly appeared to stick in his craw. Still, he didn't appear to have the patience for lingering sentimentality.

His hair was a warm, toasty brown that lightened only a little in sunlight. Square chin, rather rigid jaw, lips that could look very soft if he ever let them relax. She couldn't say he had high cheekbones. No, that wasn't what set off his eyes. That wasn't what kept her coming back to those slits of emerald, fringed with dark lashes. She'd known eyes like that once. Nicky Newman, the Don Juan of her high school days, had used eyes like Simon's to great advantage. But she was older

21

now and liked to think she couldn't be moved by such entrapments. Besides, Simon's heavy sable brows added a certain sternness to his eyes that frankly left her . . . only mildly interested. Still, if he'd smile . . .

Forget it, Joanna. He's not your type at all.

Setting the bushel basket on the dining table, she began a mental list of immediate things to do to make this new house "hers." She was already well acquainted with the furniture. Granny Sinclair had three years before willed the Early American ensemble—complete with tables, lamps, sofa and two armchairs—to Richard, who had been pronounced the most reliable caretaker among the grandchildren. Well aware that there were only two grandchildren in question, Joanna had taken the news with her usual wry aplomb.

Running a slow finger through the dust on her reading lamp, Joanna let out a resigned breath. She had to give it to Granny. Even in death, the woman had managed to state her ongoing disapproval of "Joanna's haphazard and decadent" life-style. . . .

Armed with the last of her luggage, Simon looked to the ground in contemplation as he walked to her door. He'd seen her sizing him up as though he were a side of beef. Not too many women did that to him. At least not so brazenly. She'd taken no pains to conceal her appraisal. And he'd heard her comment.

Was her *very nice* meant for him? he wondered. Well, he wasn't impressed. At least he didn't think he was. In any case, he ignored the inner smile that threatened to spread to a grin and fill his chest with warmth. She wasn't bad either, he supposed. Supposed? There was no room for supposition here. He knew. Still, there was only one way to handle a woman like her. Firmly. Entering the apartment, he set her suitcase firmly on the floor and turned to her.

"I'll be leaving now."

Turning from the basket, her gaze traveled slowly from his shoes to his eyes with the faintest pause somewhere midway before she smiled. "All right. Thanks for all the help."

Simon wanted to frown. But he didn't. What was it about her that made him want to reach down and make sure his pants were zipped? "Perhaps I should show you the kitchen first." Might as well get that out of the way, he thought. Stepping to a swinging door, he held it open in invitation. "You might want a drink or . . . something."

Feminine shoulders shrugged agreeably as she passed him. "Do you have a garden hose?"

This time Simon did frown. "Can't you just use a glass and the kitchen sink like everyone else?"

In her split second of confusion, Simon was fully aware of the finger she raised to stroke the soft skin of her throat. Although it tightened his jaw a bit, he weathered the action. He was most concerned with the full lips that pursed ever so slightly, as though she was holding back a smile. *That* bothered him.

"The hose is to fill my water bed."

"Oh. The apartment comes with beds," he defended most casually.

"Thanks, but I prefer a water bed," she said, her gaze taking in all the wide-open space of the roomy kitchen. "Ever tried one?"

"Once. The undulation kept me awake all night."

"Oh." Joanna was powerless to stop the mental picture his comment inspired. An undulating Simon Greg-

23

ory—asleep or awake—widened her eyes a bit. She looked to one blank wall, her voice suddenly breathy. "Well . . . how do you feel about nails?"

"Good God, have you tried that too? Does a regular bed hold any appeal at all?"

"I meant walls," she corrected pointedly. "Nails in walls. You see, I brought some of my favorite prints and I—"

"Oh." Simon was getting tired of saying that. He was also getting damned tired of trying to follow this woman's line of thinking. "I suppose it would be all right as long as you confine them to the paneling here in the kitchen. I have some finishing nails that will blend with the wood. When you're gone, I'll just pound them in and no one will be the wiser."

"How . . . practical," she said.

"Yes, isn't it," he agreed, oddly reassured, now that he realized how easily the reminder of Joanna Sinclair could be eradicated. Even more pleased that he had let her know it. The point made, Simon felt he could ease up a little. "Doctor—Joanna," he corrected, "if you'll move your truck to the back while I'm gone, we'll get the rest of your things this evening. Meanwhile, I hope you'll make yourself at home."

When she saw the whisper of a smile touch his lips, Joanna tried not to stare too conspicuously. "Thank you, Simon."

She watched him walk to the other side of the room where, with a jaunty push of another door, he disappeared into what she assumed was his part of the house. Joanna stared until the door stopped swinging. Finally, a hint of a thaw. But what had brought it on? Offhand, she couldn't think of a thing. But it had come just in time. She had begun to think he didn't want her around. Oh, well, maybe he'd just been waiting for some nice pictures to go in his kitchen. A doubtful smile stayed with her as she returned to the dining room and began to unpack.

Tornado Alley. That was the only term that came to mind as Simon gazed with disgust upon the ruins of his kitchen. From the looks of things, Hurricane Joanna had made a direct hit. She was fast too. He'd been gone only an hour. Stepping over a cardboard box that held a new bag of potatoes, the top half sagging rather pitifully over the side, he shook his head at the sight of plastic bowls stacked here, saucepans there. Chaos everywhere. The only order he could find in the room was a pyramid of soup cans she'd fashioned atop his refrigerator.

There were other things that deepened the creases in his furrowed brow. She had cluttered his kitchen with contraptions. An electric can opener now sat beside her microwave on the counter next to the double sink—space he'd always kept clear. His juicer had been shoved aside to make room for her popcorn popper.

There was something else too. A definite odor. Like strong peanuts. Following the scent to the table at the breakfast nook, he automatically picked up a twist tie and closed up a plastic bag of bread—white, he noted with mild disdain. Looking past another carton, his gaze lit on a case knife that stood upright, anchored in an open jumbo jar of peanut butter. His lips formed a tight line of annoyance as Simon pinched the knife between thumb and forefinger and turned to carry it to the sink. But a lingering image of dark droplets where they didn't belong brought him back to peer inside the jar.

Bits of jelly—grape, he strongly suspected—dotted the brown swirls of the peanut butter.

Simon drew a frustrated breath. Swallowing his distaste, he plunged the knife back to the jar and went to knock on her door. This wasn't going to work. Not this way, he knew. Obviously some ground rules were needed or they wouldn't survive the semester. He knocked again, more determined. Who did she think she was anyway?

There were no signs of anyone answering. Dammit, he knew she was in there. Simon pushed open the door and entered. The sight of more boxes cluttering the place he'd spent the better part of a weekend cleaning further fueled his disgust. Hands on hips, he shook his head in derision.

A husky feminine humming from the bedroom or bath—he couldn't tell which—was his only warning that she was near. Training his eyes in that general direction, Simon opened his mouth to begin the discussion. But when a wet and dripping Joanna rounded the corner, he felt his face go quite still.

During the next few seconds different parts of her body flashed in freeze frames through his mind, the images distorted like those in a Picasso painting. If a scream left the mouth she opened, he wasn't aware of it. But the shock in her eyes and the heave of creamy breasts as she took a deep involuntary breath he was aware of. Simon thought he would never forget it. He couldn't decide whether to focus on the overall picture of femininity or to zero in on exquisite details.

Joanna settled the question when she ducked behind the oval table, but not before he caught one last glimpse —also memorable—of her sleek womanly body beaded with water. The table would offer precious little shelter if he took one step to the left, he reasoned. But when her eyes, just visible between two slats of a ladder-back chair, took on a murderous gleam, Simon thought better of that.

"What are you *doing?*" she demanded.

It was a fair question. Simon knew that. "I'm sorry." He thought it best to get the apology out immediately. "I'm terribly sorry, but I thought—I knocked and you didn't answer. I thought something might be wrong. Yes, that's it. I thought you might have run into some . . . problems." His hand went up to rake the tension from his jaw in case it might be quivering. He thought it might be. Jesus, what was he thinking, barging in here like this?

"A problem?" Joanna clipped. "You seem to be the only problem *I've* run into." The room was cool and she shivered. *What* was he doing here? The question came again and again, but the answer was as elusive as the one on the Magic Eight Ball she'd played with as a child: *Reply hazy, try again later.* He was still staring, his eyes narrowed in emerald alert, his expression unreadable. "You're not some kind of weirdo, are you?"

"No." There was a split second's pause before his voice did a double take. "My God, no." Broad shoulders stiffened with his own brand of annoyance. "Why would you even think a thing like that?"

"Oh, I don't know," she said in airy anger. "I'm here, crouched behind this chair. Freezing. And you're standing there, making no effort to leave. It all adds up, somehow."

"Now, wait just a minute. I came here to talk."

As Simon stepped toward the table, she tipped her

27

chin in grave warning. "What about?" she asked, making her suspicion clear.

He moved back with a sigh. "Look, I just came in to tell you that you left your jar of peanut butter out on the table—open. And there's grape jelly in it too." His tone became oddly accusing. "Now do you really think that peanut butter and jelly belong in the same jar?"

My God. He was weird, all right. But obviously he was much more concerned with her lunch than her body. She was fully aware of the dent he'd just put in her ego and the anger it caused. Joanna's shrug was cool. She would get him for that.

"You're right, of course," she said dryly. "There's no telling what the two of them might do in there together. Why, it scares me to think about it. I mean, most of the time peanut butter is trustworthy, but jelly"—her voice dropped in sly suspicion—"you really have to keep an eye on jelly."

Simon looked away, the rise and fall of his chest apparent beneath his shirt. But he said nothing.

"As long as you're here, could you get me a towel from one of the cans behind you?" she asked with studied nonchalance. "And that big bottle of shampoo. I believe they're in the one by the sofa."

So that was why she was traipsing through the house like that. Simon turned to fulfill her request, thinking all the time that if she'd possessed an ounce of foresight none of this would have happened. "Obviously, you're a woman who never thinks ahead," he observed dryly, rummaging through her belongings.

"Maybe," she admitted. "I like to think I'm spontaneous and given to impulse. You might as well know that right off the bat."

28

"Yes, well, there are a few things *you* should know right off the bat," he returned, grimacing at the use of a trite cliché.

"Fine. But could all this wait until I've showered and dressed?"

She made good sense. Placing the towel and shampoo on the table, Simon stood away again. "Of course," he said, turning his back to the clear demand in the lift of her brows.

Rising to reach for the towel, Joanna kept an eye on Simon as he walked to the door. When he turned back saying, "Joanna," she shot behind the table again and groaned.

"Sorry," he offered, frustration evident in his voice. "I just wanted to say that I know we can work things out. Everything will be fine after we set some ground rules. I do want you to be comfortable here."

"Just go."

"Right now," she heard him mumble. "I'm going right now."

But after he had gone, Joanna didn't get up right away. She was too intrigued by the last few minutes to move just yet. Comfortable? *This* was comfortable? Here she was on all fours, feeling much like a wet dog trying to get in the back door. Unfolding her stiff limbs to a standing position, Joanna got the full effect of the air conditioner. But even as she shivered and reached for the towel to wrap around herself, a knowing smile played at one corner of her mouth.

So, he wanted her to be comfortable. Well, she fully intended to be. But he wanted ground rules too. It didn't make sense. Comfort and rules were totally incompatible. With a sigh, Joanna tossed the bottle of shampoo in the air and caught it, then took up her humming again as she made her way back to the bathroom.

CHAPTER TWO

"Have you seen much of her yet?"

In the entryway Simon hesitated, not knowing quite how to answer Stan Farber's question. Not more than five minutes had passed since he'd seen quite a lot of her. "Not much," he answered, taking another sip of his drink. "Dr. Sinclair only arrived this afternoon—as you know."

Leading the way past the wide stairs and into the living room, Simon stood at the fireplace and wondered what had brought the chairman of the Sociology Department. At the meeting earlier Stan had mentioned nothing about coming by.

"On your way to the courts?" he asked, unaccountably put off by the tennis whites that exposed Farber's tanned, muscular thighs. Joanna was sure to be impressed by that.

"Yeah, that's right." After a surreptitious glance around the room as though he were expecting someone else, Stan sat on the sofa and crossed a sneakered foot over one knee. "Thought you might like to come along. My regular partner skipped out on me for a weekend in St. Louis."

"Sorry, but I don't play." A fairly well-known fact among the *entire* faculty, Simon suspected, hardly aware that he was loosening his tie.

"Too bad." The dark-haired man seemed not at all troubled by the news, leaning back to rest one arm comfortably along the edge of the tuxedo sofa while the other hand preened a neat moustache.

"Would you like a drink?"

"Sure." Stan nodded agreeably. "Scotch if you have it."

Simon walked behind the bar and began to fix the drink. Pouring the amber liquid over ice, he noticed Stan's more relaxed perusal of the room and its bookcases lining one wall.

"You've really changed the place since . . . Susan left."

"Some," Simon admitted, placing the scotch on the small marble-top table beside the sofa. "I guess it's more in line with my tastes now."

"Yeah. Susan was a little flighty. And you . . . you're sort of somber."

Simon frowned slightly, taking the chair opposite his guest. "I don't think that fairly characterizes either one of us," he defended casually, and then finished off his drink.

"Maybe not, but you have to admit you've become awfully serious this past year. Personally, I think you could've used the sabbatical more than Richard." Stan looked down, beginning to twirl the aglet on his shoe-lace. "So, how do you like it?"

"How do I like what?"

"Having a woman in the house again."

Simon let out a deep breath, and got up to make himself another drink. "I wish you wouldn't put it that way," he said, dropping more ice cubes into his glass. "We're not really in the same house."

"For all practical purposes, you *are.*"

Simon thought about that for a moment, wondering why Stan's knowing smirk made him feel uneasy. "To be honest, I'm not sure I'm going to like it."

"Why? I think it'll be good for you," Stan responded with another unwelcome comment. "Since the divorce, you've done nothing but work. But now that the book's finished, you can think about more pleasant things. Get back in the groove. Live a little. And what better way than with a woman?"

On its way to the glass a bit of bourbon sloshed onto the bar, further irritating Simon. "I've been doing exactly what I wanted to do." After blotting the spill with a folded bar towel, he returned to his chair.

"Personally, I can't imagine anything quite as dry as an economics textbook." Stan stared into his glass. "I've heard a lot about her."

"Who?"

A patient smile meandered to the mouth beneath the moustache. "Joanna Sinclair—or Dr. Sinclair, as you call her. Does she call you Dr. Gregory?" Stan asked, but didn't wait for a reply. "When do you think you'll drop the formalities?" he said dryly.

"I hardly think it matters what we call each other as long as she receives the respect she and her title deserve," Simon replied, although he was uncertain himself about the exact amount that would entail.

"Don't get me wrong," Stan said, lifting a reassuring palm. "I have respect for her. I hear she's a great speaker. And her articles on consumer scams are always right on the mark. But the one on higher education in private colleges and universities—now that was fantastic."

It was hardly the word Simon would have used for that particular syndicated piece. "She brought up a few pertinent questions," he conceded. "But I'm not sure that criticizing education is a proper subject for a consumer advocate."

"Students are consumers of our services, Simon. But that's neither here nor there." Stan shrugged his mild indifference, his voice lowering to a growl—a ridiculous growl to Simon's ears: "All I know is that she must be one sharp lady, rather liberal in her attitudes, if you know what I mean, and I intend to be on a first-name basis with her at the first opportunity."

Damn, he was smug, Simon thought. Stan would probably sidle right up to her and give her some clever line—the way he did with every attractive woman he met—and she would fall all over herself, loving every minute of it. He thought he might hate this particular woman if she succumbed. For some reason that he didn't even want to know, Simon decided to delay that moment as long as possible. The matter settled, he sipped his drink and pushed the thought from his mind.

Stan reached down to pull his white knit socks back to his calves. "I'd love to meet her."

"Who?" Simon asked, deliberately obtuse.

"Joanna."

34

"You will, Stan." The host stood, hoping the guest would take his cue and make some move to leave. "Let's give her some time to get settled."

"Aren't you being awfully protective?" Nevertheless, the man set his glass down and rose. "What's she like?"

"Oh, you know. What you might expect from Richard's sister."

"That bad, huh." Stan delivered a teasing fist to Simon's shoulder. "Pretty?"

"In a short sort of way, I suppose. If you like that type."

"What type is that?"

"Oh, I don't know. She's . . . lively."

"I like that type."

"Well, not lively, really." Simon's amendment was immediate as he continued edging his way to the door, his voice—and the subject matter, he suspected—luring Stan along with him. "Actually, she's more disorganized than anything else. Maybe lazy would be a better word. Yes, I think it would be."

"Why do you say that?"

"Well, she . . . does strange things with food."

Stan's eyes widened. "She does?" he asked, a smile beginning to tilt his mouth.

Momentarily distracted by a clattering sound from the kitchen, Simon nodded absently, certain that Stan must have heard it also. "Yes, with trash cans too."

"Oh, my God." The words were mumbled so softly that Simon wasn't sure he'd heard.

"Well, Stan, I'm glad you dropped by. Come again soon." Simon opened the door, but Stan refused to leave.

"I forgot," he said quickly. "You said you'd lend me

your copy of *Catcher in the Rye*. I'd like it now, if you don't mind."

"Of course not." Simon kept his eyes focused on Stan. But his thoughts were on the kitchen door. He wanted badly to get in there and see what was happening. See her. Just out of curiosity, he told himself firmly. Nothing more.

"Well?" Stan prompted.

"Well, what?" Then Simon remembered. "The book's in the bedroom. Wait right here while I get it." But Simon knew Stan wouldn't wait. Sounds of the other man's squeaky heels on the hardwood floor began almost immediately. Damn, where was that book?

Before he even began the search in the bedroom at the back of the house, Simon heard the faint knock on his kitchen door. And then a feminine, "Are you decent?"

"Never," came Stan's smooth reply and Simon cringed.

In the kitchen Joanna frowned slightly at Simon's sudden playfulness. She shrugged. "Okay, I've got my clothes on now and I'm ready to talk."

As Joanna swung open the door and—uumph—entered the room, she was startled by the unfamiliar man who stood, both palms forming a pyramid over his nose. Tears appeared to be gathering in his eyes. She couldn't really tell because he turned away so fast, doubling over as he did so. He seemed to be taking deep breaths too. "Hello," she said, concern lifting her brows. "Is anything wrong?"

The rather nasal "No, everything's fine" he offered brought deep, satisfied laughter from the bedroom door, where Simon stood, green eyes crinkling nicely at the corners. She thought he looked very appealing when he did that. And his eyes stayed that way even though he reluctantly cut short the sounds of amusement beneath the other man's glare.

Joanna self-consciously patted the terry-cloth towel, wrapped turban-style around her head. "Am I interrupting anything?"

"I think your timing was perfect," Simon said, stepping forward. "Joanna, meet Stan Farber. He's head of Sociology at Houghton. Stan, Dr. Joanna Sinclair."

"How nice," she said, holding out a hand to the man.

Stan Farber let go of his nose long enough to shake her hand. But Joanna noticed he sniffed shortly a few times. Bad sinuses, she decided, offering a smile. "Have you been at Houghton long?"

"Two years," came the reply. The hint of a twang was still present, but Stan went right on, letting his voice drop seductively, Simon noticed, mentally shaking his head. "How long will we have the pleasure of your company?"

Joanna turned her face, smiling so prettily that for two cents Simon would have reached out and whipped the towel right off her head to expose what he knew would be a mass of wet—unattractive—tangles.

"Only for the semester, unfortunately," she said, fully aware of her extremely casual appearance at that moment. The mismatched red sweat shirt and purple jogging pants had been handy, and since Simon had seemed in such a hurry to talk . . . well, apparently this nice-looking man didn't care. "I'm sure I'll enjoy my time here," she added congenially.

"Hey," Stan said with a sly smile, "if there are any problems, you just let old Stan the Fan know about it."

Something was definitely hitting the fan or getting deeper, Simon didn't know which. He stepped between the mutual admiration society, forcing both Stan and Joanna to put some distance between themselves. "Here," he said, swinging the edge of the book into Stan's flat stomach. Then Simon's hands went into his pockets as he nodded amiably. "Isn't this nice. You two look so—athletic. Here's old Stan in stunning tennis togs." Turning to Joanna, Simon smiled. "And I must say I admire the fashion risk *you're* taking."

A slow warmth crept up her neck as Joanna aimed her sweetest smile at Simon. "Why, thank you." It must be something in the air that gave good moods such a short life-span in this house, she mused angrily. But Simon ignored her wilting look.

"Stan was just leaving," he went on.

But the man wouldn't budge, holding out his hand again for Joanna to take. "I look forward to seeing you at the faculty reception on Thursday," he said, "if not sooner."

"Well, thank you, but I try to avoid that sort of thing. Receptions are usually so"—Joanna wrinkled her nose in apology—"snooty."

Stan's moustache seemed to droop in mild disappointment. "But this reception is in your honor. I arranged everything."

She forced her face to straighten. "How . . . wonderful."

"You seem surprised. Didn't Simon tell you?" he asked, sparing a split second's accusing glance toward the guilty party.

"I'm sure we'll discuss it at length," Joanna said evenly, slipping her hand from his.

"I must say I prefer something a little less pretentious too." Then, with a wink, he added, "I know we can work something out."

Joanna shrugged easily, not nearly so certain of that possibility.

"Until then—*Joanna.*"

She gave him one last smile and hoped that he would go before her face froze in that position.

The moment he had turned the corner out of her sight, Joanna pivoted and strolled back to the kitchen, preferring to meet Simon on "neutral turf." She put away the peanut butter first, since that seemed to be the one thing that could throw him into a tailspin. When he entered the room, she was holding the bag of potatoes, wondering what to do with it.

"In the cabinet to the left of the stove," he said, letting the door swing closed.

"What?"

"The potatoes. In the cabinet."

"Thanks," she said stiffly and followed his direction.

When she turned back to him, Simon was reaching to the inside pocket of his jacket to pull out a small square envelope. "Your invitation to the reception. Sorry I didn't give it to you sooner, but you have to admit things have been slightly . . . disorganized since you arrived."

"Somehow I get the feeling you're about to change all that." Joanna took the envelope and placed it temporarily on the table at the breakfast nook. "Is this 'talk' going to be a formal affair?" she asked, glancing down at her outfit.

She watched him draw a deep breath in answer, setting his jaw on "tough" for her benefit. "I can talk no matter what you're wearing."

True, she admitted in stubborn remembrance. He could talk even when she was wearing nothing at all. "I could use some coffee. Go ahead and say what you have to say while I make some." She began to rummage through the box nearest the refrigerator for the coffee maker. Richard didn't drink the stuff. Luckily she'd remembered to bring hers.

Taking a seat at the table, Simon didn't say anything for a minute. He was caught up in watching Joanna, although he tried his damnedest not to. She had compact hips judging from the mildest jiggle beneath the knit material as she moved. When she bent to the box again, the hem of her sweat shirt rode up to reveal a small waist and a short length of feminine spine. Spines were neither feminine nor masculine, he reminded himself firmly. Still, hers definitely had a delicate feminine look about it.

As she straightened, he wondered if the material would drop back into place and thereby shut him out. It remained hitched up. He was oddly pleased. She had a freckle just to the left of one intricate vertebra. He began to count the tiny exposed sections of her spine. The number came to three. He wondered how many more he would find below the waist of her jogging pants if he . . . Drawing himself up short, Simon looked away. When he restlessly began drumming his fingertips on the tabletop, she turned to him, brows lifted.

"Go ahead. I'm listening."

The precursory clearing of his throat was not so helpful as he might have wished. "I'll just wait until you're finished."

With a shrug she continued to assemble all the makings for coffee on a patch of clear counter space. When the pot was prepared and the cord plugged into the nearest outlet, a barefoot Joanna took a chair opposite him. "I'm all yours."

There was his jaw going all hard again, she noticed, wishing the man would relax. She tried a small smile. "Ummm. There's nothing better than the smell of good coffee brewing. By the way, I didn't see your pot out anywhere. You're welcome to use mine anytime."

"I drink one cup of hot tea every morning."

"One?" she teased. "No more? No less?"

Seeing the attractive tilt of her chin, he suddenly wished he had lied, just so he *could* use something that belonged to her. But he saw nothing wise in that. "Just one," he said, closing the door to that particular subject. "Now. What time do you usually have your dinner?"

Joanna merely stared a moment, never having thought much about it, never having found that part of her life noteworthy. "No particular time. Whenever I get hungry."

"Really? I find myself starving by seven-thirty," he confessed. "I like to start cooking my dinner about six-thirty, so if you could have yours over by then, I'd—"

"It takes you an hour to throw something together? You could use the microwave and—"

"I don't *throw* anything together," he said evenly. "But thanks anyway. If you'll just load the dishwasher when you're finished, I'll turn it on after I clean up. And you're free to use the dishes and cookware. In fact, all the equipment in here is at your disposal." He paused as though waiting for her comment.

Already planning secret, supplemental midnight

41

snacks, Joanna deferred to him. "Go ahead. I think you're on a roll."

Answering the soft sarcasm with a pointed stare at the square tiles of the floor, Simon continued, "You can use the cabinet by the stove for canned goods. I'll move your microwave over there too. And of course you'll need space in the refrigerator—"

"The freezer, mostly," she corrected.

His head came up in mild wonder. "No fresh fruits and vegetables?" he asked with such innocence that she held back the smile she knew was forming.

"I don't eat many of those."

"Don't you worry about things like . . . beriberi?"

"Not much." The smile burst forth, pushing its way guilelessly to her mouth, bringing with it a helpless chuckle. "Not any more than scurvy scurvy."

Green eyes narrowed considerably and, going with the sudden impulse, Joanna screwed up her mouth to glare playfully back at him.

He drew in a deep breath at that and slowly let it out again. "I take a shower first thing in the morning. Every morning."

"I never doubted it for a moment." Slipping the towel from her head, she began to rake her fingers slowly through the dark tangles.

"I tell you that only because Richard and I sometimes had a problem with hot water."

"I'll remember. Anything else?"

Watching her fingers repeatedly glide in sensuous treks through her hair, Simon raised a palm to the back of his neck, putting an end to the slightest tingle there. "Yes," he said. Moving to the wall on the opposite side of the room, he opened louvered walnut doors to expose

42

a washer and dryer. "I do my laundry on Thursday evenings. Is that all right with you?" Resting his arms against his broad chest, Simon leaned against the edge of the dryer.

When he also crossed one foot over the other, Joanna was curiously heartened. It was the most casual move he'd made in her short acquaintance with him. Confining her gaze to the decorative perforations on the toe of his shoe, she found herself admiring the way his trousers hugged—but not too tightly—the pleasing lines of a thoroughly masculine physique. Thinking it best not to provoke him, she smiled, all the while knowing that preserving his pleasant disposition was not her only motive. "Fine."

He seemed to want further comment. When she made none, he frowned. "Well, aren't you going to tell me when you prefer to do *your* laundry?"

She opened her mouth to speak, but he cut her off. "I know, whenever you feel like it," he said, shaking his head in mild disapproval.

"Right," she said, nodding hers.

"Well, I hope you won't do any washing without a full load."

"Full loads only," she swore, wondering absently if there was any rule about playing without a full deck. Upon further consideration, she withdrew the question. The man was simply overly faithful to schedules, overly serious about his kitchen. About everything. But she was becoming rather restless with the details. "Is that all?"

"Yes, I think so."

"Good. I'll say one thing, Simon. You're nothing if

not consistent. But tell me, are there any unplanned moments in your life?"

Several, he thought. All of them occurring within the space of this one afternoon. But offhand he couldn't think of one such moment that he could tell her about, even though he wanted badly to come up with something if only to dispel the honest concern in the blue gaze that now probed him mercilessly. "I simply find my life easier if I have a certain amount of order in it," he defended.

She shifted sideways in the chair to fully face him. Drawing her knees up to rest beneath her chin, she entwined her fingers in an easy—and damned provocative —embrace of shapely calves.

"Do you always keep such a strict routine?" she asked.

"Do you—" Simon stopped himself. He would *not* ask if she *always* painted her toenails. In the first place, it was none of his business. In the second place—no, make it first—he didn't want to know any intimate details about her. "Do you have any kind of routine at all?" he countered.

The gruff question surprised and irked her. "I try not to get bogged down in that sort of thing," she said tartly.

Pulling the louvered doors together, he returned to the chair to sit again. "The only thing that really matters is that we cooperate with each other."

It didn't seem as though he merely wanted her to cooperate. It looked more like total surrender to her. But she swallowed that feeling for now. "I'm the tenant. You're the landlord. I'm not sure all these rules are necessary, but I'll abide by them—whenever possible.

All things considered, maybe it's best if we try to stay out of each other's way."

"I wish you wouldn't put it like that."

"Oh?" she asked, lowering her feet to the floor in challenge. "How would you have me put it?"

"Why, we're going to observe the rules of common courtesy, that's all. Give each other the privacy we deserve."

She leaned forward to goad. "Privacy?"

He leaned forward too, his chin dipping in mild warning. "I've already apologized for interrupting your bath."

"You did," she admitted grudgingly.

"So I see nothing to get angry about."

"I'm not angry," she assured candidly, getting up to pour herself a cup of coffee. She was frustrated more than anything else. Frustrated with both the "kitchen accord" and Simon's attitude. Joanna considered herself a spontaneous, free-spirited, friendly person who enjoyed people. It wasn't that she merely disliked unnecessary schedules. She abhorred them and couldn't think why some people imposed them upon themselves with such vigor.

The sip of hot coffee wasn't the only thing that burned as she took to the chair again. The truth was that she found him attractive, despite his meticulous habits, despite his deep devotion to rules. But Simon obviously found her . . . a mess. That unflattering fact nudged itself stubbornly among the other minor annoyances she felt.

Nevertheless, she had conceded to Simon for the time being. Now it was his turn, she mused. Following his example, Joanna relaxed against her chair in preparation for the next round.

"There's just one more thing," she ventured. "Do you think it might be possible to schedule my classes to begin around ten o'clock in the morning?" She saw his head come up in certain denial. Joanna sped ahead. "You see, I'm what's called a night person. I do my best work in the evenings. Sometimes I don't go to bed until dawn. As a result I like to sleep late. Is there anything you can do?" He was the chairman of Economics after all.

"Absolutely not."

She waited for further explanation. At least some polite excuse for vetoing her request. Neither was forthcoming. "Why not?" she asked, beginning to regret giving in to his demands so easily.

"Because I have nothing to do with the scheduling of classes," he said matter-of-factly.

"Have you no influence?"

"Of course, but I wouldn't abuse it by asking special consideration just for the purpose of allowing you to sleep late. Houghton isn't run that way." Then, as though he couldn't quite believe she'd asked, a smug smile tugged at his mouth. "Night person," he whispered with a shake of his head. "That's a good one."

Indignance stiffened her shoulders as she stood. "You know, I find your attitude quite provincial, Simon—on several levels. Contrary to what you may believe, some of us simply don't function at our full potential before midmorning."

"On the other hand, some of us never function at our full potential," he returned smoothly. "But if that's your problem, please don't make it Houghton's."

Joanna had a faint desire to show him the full potential of her fist set against the background of his attractive jaw. But she didn't. Joanna didn't hit men. Generally, it gave them too much incentive to hit back. Besides, she could take defeat as gracefully as the next person—certainly better than the one next to her now, she suspected. "As I told you before, the only problem I've run into is you," she said, letting the dispassion of her tone trickle into her expression. "Now, I think I'll get to work."

"Good idea." Simon stood to remove his jacket, fitting it around the back of his chair. "Shall we get the rest of your things from the truck?"

"If you're sure I won't be intruding on your privacy." She dropped the comment over one shoulder as though it were a scented hankie and then continued toward the back door, a small smile tugging at her irritation. He might be picky. He might be terribly serious. But she suspected that he might also be very passionate under all the layers of solemnity. That intrigued her.

Aware that he was following, albeit slowly, Joanna couldn't help thinking that her time at Houghton College might prove to be the most interesting four and a half months she'd spent in a great while.

CHAPTER THREE

"What's a nice girl like you . . ."

Joanna closed her mind to the rest of Stan Farber's line, letting it blend with the low hum of conversation in the room. Sipping her coffee, she stood a few yards from the foamy punch bowl, contemplating her third trip to the buffet and the tempting selection of canapés and sweets there. She shouldn't—but she would if he didn't say something original soon.

"Why don't we blow this joint?" he whispered close to her ear.

Joanna smiled a gentle reprimand. "That wouldn't be very polite. Our hosts have gone to a lot of trouble—"

Stan waved away her excuses. "The Hamptons wouldn't mind at all. George and Mimi are the most laid-back professors we've got."

George and Mimi. George and Mimi. Joanna rolled the names over in her mind, hoping they would stay there. They were almost the only ones that had, she'd met so many people during the past hour. Simon had brought her to the reception and then politely dumped her, apparently feeling he'd fulfilled his obligation to the guest of honor.

In a way, she was grateful to Stan for latching on to her. Despite his inane comments, he had rescued her memory several times. And he seemed to know and admire her work in consumer affairs, even if he had bored more than one guest with a thorough rundown of her career.

"There's a film festival going on at Claymore Hall right now," he suggested. "W. C. Fields. What do you think?"

"I think I'll have another piece of fudge." She patted the sleeve of his jacket in apology. "Thanks anyway, Stan."

On her way to the chocolate end of the table, Joanna spotted Simon again. He was standing in a group near the bar, obviously in full command of a conversation with two men and a very attractive blonde. Swallowing the envy in her throat, Joanna surreptitiously plucked two pieces of fudge from the platter and moved on to the coffee urn. The man was spewing more words this evening than she'd heard from him during the last seven days combined.

At first his suggestion that they come to the reception in one car had pleased her. She hadn't seen much of Simon the past few days, except for accidental meetings in the kitchen. He never tarried. But God, she would have loved the chance to tell him about her first week at Houghton. After only one day of teaching, she'd mentioned her unexpected enthusiasm for the job. He had merely nodded, smiling politely, as though he'd fully expected her reaction. Joanna sighed inwardly at the frustration of that.

Lately, she'd felt a strong urge to paint Richard's bathroom. That's what she would have done at home to combat the restlessness she was experiencing these days. But Richard's bathroom was papered with a rather expensive-looking foil and so, for her brother's sake, she'd resisted.

Her cup filled, Joanna made her way to a spinet piano, where she chewed on a square of fudge and continued her covert observation of Simon. In addition to being a great conversationalist, he was obviously a good listener, if the attention he now paid the blonde was any indication. The woman took full advantage, leaning close to him, touching his jacket sleeve now and then as she spoke. Every once in a while, she gave his arm a little squeeze. Joanna popped the second piece of candy into her mouth and chewed vigorously.

Although Simon offered no outward encouragement of the contact, neither did he avoid it, she noted. Joanna couldn't blame the blonde. Simon, with his tall good looks and his unfailing courtesy, was a definite challenge to any red-blooded woman. Of all the men in the room, he was clearly the Grand Prize. The aloof charm he exuded only made him more coveted. His features were neither very dark nor very light, but rather an alluring combination of what she would call . . . toasty.

She turned deliberately away from all that allure in time to assure Mimi Hampton—a striking redhead who continually fussed with the neckline of a low-cut blouse —that the guest of honor was having a wonderful time and that the entire evening was going beautifully.

"Thanks," Mimi said, letting her smile of perpetual worry lapse for the moment. "I hope Stan didn't embarrass you too much by asking you to say a few words to the group. He's a little . . . well, a little . . ."

"Overwhelming?" Joanna supplied.

Mimi pointed an agreeable finger. "Right." Then the hostess turned away to look after another guest.

Joanna took the now familiar path to the buffet and scanned the array of delicacies. Mentally thumbing her nose at the raw cauliflower, carrots and dip, she reached for the fudge again.

"Don't you think you've had enough?" It was Simon leaning over her shoulder in droll accusation.

She smiled. "It's all right. I'm not driving." Aware of the tangy male scent that now pleased her senses, Joanna sneaked a deep breath of it into her lungs. Nice, very nice, she admitted. "Enjoying yourself?"

"Yes, I like seeing colleagues in a social setting now and then."

"Um." Joanna sipped her coffee. "Is the blonde a colleague?"

"Gina? The one in the pretty green dress?" He nodded. "She's the cosmetology instructor."

"Ah. Gina, the cosmetologist." He hadn't even mentioned *her* dress, a polka-dotted holdover from the forties, complete with padded shoulders, fitted waist and a bias-cut skirt—the works, including matching two-toned pumps. "I don't believe I've met her," Joanna said, positioning her ankle for a vain glance of navy and white leather uppers.

"I offered to introduce the two of you, but Gina preferred to wait. Perhaps she's a little in awe."

"I'm almost sure of it." Joanna turned a patient smile up at him. "But I doubt I'm the object of her awe."

He ignored that. "I found her rather shy."

Joanna found him rather naive. But she didn't say so. It was all part of his charm, she supposed. "Like my new dress, Simon?"

After a moment's hesitation, he took one step backward. What followed was a thoroughly masculine perusal of her overall appearance from head to toe. He seemed to take the matter quite seriously, allowing nothing to escape his notice. Now that she had his undivided attention, Joanna found herself flushing beneath his penetrating gaze, wondering if he had any deepseated dislike for the era her dress represented. "A simple yes or no will do."

Slowly he met her eyes again. "Pretty. It reminds me of my mother."

She sighed. "How nice."

"I meant it as a compliment," he said calmly.

"I'm sure you did." But the compliment simply didn't take. She'd expected more from such close scrutiny on the part of a single man. And from the money she'd spent. Still, she had asked—had *had* to ask—another fact that rankled her. "Tell me something, Simon. How long were you married?"

"Two years," he said, reaching for a carrot stick. "Why?"

"No reason. I just thought it might've been longer."

"Why? Because I seem settled?"

"Entrenched might be a better word." Ignoring the questioning lift of his brow, Joanna let curiosity lure her deeper into the more personal topic. "Did your wife dress to suit you?"

52

His answer was candid and succinct. "Yes. Susan liked the challenge of putting an outfit together. She could look at an article of clothing in a store window and know instantly whether or not it coordinated with what she had at home. She had excellent taste in that area."

Joanna merely nodded, wishing she had left the subject of his ex-wife alone. She, herself, didn't buy dresses. She bought entire windows. That very afternoon a slinky mannequin in a local boutique had been stripped bare of everything—including earbobs, bracelet and a rolled-up score of "I Won't Dance, Don't Ask Me"—for this occasion. The nylon mesh rat had been left at home only because Joanna couldn't figure out how to get her hair around it. She wasn't a mix 'n matcher who could pick up a scarf here, a belt there and somehow make it all come together—not like Susan, obviously. When all was said and done, Joanna guessed she just didn't coordinate without help. She accepted that, operating on the theory that any complaints could damn well be directed to an obscure window dresser. Anyway, she only wore dresses when nothing else would do, and most usually for men. Why else would she wear them? Slacks and jeans were much more to her taste.

"Nervous, Joanna?"

She swung an expression of curt denial up at him. "Of course not. Why?"

With the slightest lift of his broad shoulders Simon shrugged his doubt. "You seem rather preoccupied. Is anything wrong?"

She followed his gaze to her palm, where four pieces of fudge had mysteriously collected. Her eyes went wide for a moment, but she recovered quickly. "Nothing wrong here," she insisted, and then one by one replaced the pieces of candy on the platter, stacking the pieces in careful pyramid formation. "There now, isn't that better?" she asked with a brisk dust of her hands.

"Much," he agreed dryly, and then cupped her arm to steer her away from further temptation. "Now that you've been teaching for almost a week, what do you think of Houghton?" he asked, halting near a secluded alcove.

Her mood brightened immediately now that he'd broached a subject that interested her. "It's been wonderful," she said with positive assurance. "Absolutely wonderful. So far, everything's gone off without a hitch. Those students are there to learn, Simon. Really learn. Very bright. I think I can work with them."

"Good news," he said absently, his casual gaze scanning the roomful of guests, "considering that you committed yourself to that purpose at least two months ago."

"Oh, but I had my doubts," she admitted. "I mean I've never done this before. But, yes, I think I can do something with them."

Suspicion clouded the glance he spared her. "Just what did you have in mind?"

Joanna took that as a definite invitation. "Some projects, special studies, you know—for extra credit. I can't wait."

Simon drew a deep breath and gave her his full attention. "Now, Joanna, I think the study plan is very clear. For good reason," he added cautiously.

"Of course," she agreed, wondering what she had said to make him stiffen up as he had. "I know that a certain amount of material has to be covered during the semester. But surely there's room for innovation on the instructor's part. Some enthusiasm. Don't you think so?"

"I think you're a temporary teacher, Joanna—for one semester. Until Richard comes back. Your experience is limited." His shrug was thoughtfully impatient. "No, let's be honest. Your experience is nonexistent, despite your credentials. I hope you'll do the job you were hired to do. No more. No less. Got that?"

She frowned her dissent and her irritation. "You don't want me to encourage them?"

"Encouragement is admirable, but—"

"I want to get on their wavelength, Simon. In another week, I'll have them telling me their wildest aspirations."

"Why would you want to *know* their wildest aspirations? It isn't wise to get too friendly with students."

"That's ridiculous. How can you create a comfortable atmosphere by maintaining a distance between yourself and them? I *want* to be friends with them. If I'm going to be good, I'll have to give of myself completely."

"Yes, well, I'd venture to say that your male students will be ecstatic about your attitude."

The remark took away her breath momentarily. Nevertheless, Joanna smiled through her anger. "Why, Simon, it isn't like you to put things on such a physical level. I'm surprised."

"Well, don't be. I haven't forgotten what it was like to be eighteen and running loose on a college campus—"

"Ah, you sly devil."

"—and you really know very little about what I'm like," he returned. "Some students are like maggots in

55

hot ashes. They're into everything at first. They have no focus, no direction."

"That may or may not be true," she conceded. "I don't believe they're all that scattered. My students seem to know exactly where they're going. If I can help them get there, then—"

"The point I'm trying to make is that sometimes that distance you mentioned is what gives us the advantage we need to keep things running smoothly."

Breathing rather heavily now, Joanna looked away, trying to regain control. Richard's bathroom, wallpaper or not, was beginning to look damned tempting. "You're entitled to your opinion. I'm entitled to mine." Damn him. She should have known he'd be the first to douse her ideas with cold logic. She wasn't even going to tell him about her plan to invite her honors class over for a backyard barbecue before the weather became too cold. That would only invite more disagreement.

Joanna was glad when Stan appeared to relieve the impasse between her and Simon.

"Have you changed your mind?" he asked, his sidelong whisper effectively excluding Simon from the question. Although Simon studied his shoes, she knew he was listening carefully.

"You know, Stan," she replied, "I think I'll take you up on your invitation after all. Suddenly, W. C. Fields appeals to me very much."

"Great. We can catch the last two movies if we go now."

"I'm ready any time you are."

Stan looked oddly pleased, as though he couldn't decide whether it was his charm or his good looks that had persuaded her. Joanna hadn't the heart to tell him that Simon's pompous attitude had convinced her that the party was over. She only wished Stan would be a little more subtle about his victory.

"Good night, Simon," she offered civilly. "I'm sure Stan will take me home."

Watching the two of them say good night to the Hamptons, Simon tried hard to control his irritation at what he saw as blatant rudeness. He stood rigid until Joanna and Stan had gone and then walked to a wide window, where he stared out into the Thursday darkness. The guest of honor had left halfway through the reception. That made him angry—that and his faint disappointment that he wouldn't be taking her home after all. Until now he hadn't realized that he'd looked forward to that event. He pushed his tense hands into his trouser pockets. It wasn't the first time he'd gone home alone, he told himself.

His thoughts forged ahead with speculation about what time she'd arrive home. Probably not until very late. Maybe not at all. She was a grown woman. But as Simon stepped up to the bar and requested a bourbon, neat, he couldn't help wondering if there was any subtle way he could bring up the subject of a curfew with his temporary tenant. No, he conceded, lifting the glass to his lips. It wouldn't work. She would scratch his eyes out first.

By the time Stan pulled his car into her driveway at the back of the house, the long day had caught up with Joanna. Several late nights and early mornings had left her yearning for the weekend and the chance to sleep until noon if she chose to. One more day, she thought. Then she would have it made. At the moment, though, she looked forward to a good book, her bed and, most of all, some temporary rejuvenation. Noting the bounce in Stan's step as he walked her to her door and opened it, Joanna thought it wise to advise him of her plan immediately.

"Thanks for a wonderful evening, Stan. If it weren't so late I'd invite you in for a cup of coffee."

Apparently he didn't care about her plan. He closed the door and came to stand very close to her, his thigh brushing the edge of the kitchen table.

"Do you think Simon's home yet?" Before she could respond with her "Maybe" Stan slipped his hand to her waist in casual intimacy. "He didn't look too pleased when we left the party early. Did you see that chin of his dip into stern disapproval?" Stan asked with a conspiratorial chuckle, and then imitated the expression.

Joanna didn't know why her shoulders slowly drew up in offense. She was amazed that they had, really. But the remark worked its way under her skin like a pesky splinter. She felt a certain peeve at having Simon mocked in her presence, even though she'd done it often in private the past few days. That was all right, though, she defended. Her mockery was more affectionate—she surprised herself with that word. It was true, though. She did feel a certain detached affection for her landlord. Even their disagreements were entertaining. She wanted Stan to leave so that she could think about it more.

"I have an early day tomorrow, Stan."

"I know." But he made no move to release her. "Wouldn't it be a cozier night if I stayed and together we helped that old sun come up?"

"Somehow I think that old sun can manage without

any help from us," she said wryly, wondering how he came up with all the roundabout ways to say "Let's go to bed." She preferred the more direct approach, thereby allowing a more direct refusal.

"I could sneak out early in the morning. No one would ever know I was here."

No one, meaning Simon, no doubt. "If you were to stay—which you are not," she reaffirmed, "you certainly wouldn't have to sneak out. I haven't lived with my mother for quite some time."

"Right," he admitted dryly. "Now you've got Simon. He's more strict than any mother I know."

There it was again, she thought. The mockery. Joanna liked it less and less. But when Stan drew her into his arms with the clear intent of kissing her, she didn't fight it. To her mind, the action signaled an end —not one that she particularly relished—but an end nonetheless to the evening. Stan, however, apparently saw it as a great beginning.

His moist lips seemed to be all over her mouth, his tongue flicking as though working against time. Her hands resting lightly on his shoulders, Joanna allowed the kiss to last for another moment, his moustache tickling her upper lip until she muffled a giggle. Well aware that his thumbs on her waist had begun to circle upward to the undersides of her breasts, she frowned and then firmly pushed against his hold on her. That seemed to be Stan's cue to explore further. He pulled her back into his clutches and tried very hard to kiss her again. She bent backward to avoid another unwanted licking.

"All right, *Octo*-Stan," she said with a chuckle and then wriggled free of his grasp. "I think we'd better say good night. And thanks for the movie."

With a look of intense frustration on his face, he raised his hand to smoothe his moustache.

A deep clearing of a masculine throat swung her gaze to Simon, who stood on the other side of the room, hands thrust into pockets as he peered intently into an open cabinet as though in search of the Holy Grail. In long shirt-sleeves, no tie and no shoes, he took a glass from the shelf and closed the door. When he turned to her and Stan, his attitude appeared casual.

"Ah, hello, Stan, Joanna." But there was nothing casual in the eyes that flashed anger as he moved to the sink and twisted the cold-water handle to send water thundering from the spigot into his glass. When the tap was silent, Simon raised the filled glass to his lips and faced them again, but didn't look directly at either.

"How was the film festival?"

"Great." Oblivious to Simon's clipped tone, Stan shifted to drape a heavy arm around Joanna's shoulder. "But then W. C. Fields is always funny. We enjoyed ourselves immensely."

"How nice."

Joanna's palms went together in a self-conscious rub as she moved away from Stan. She didn't know exactly why Simon was irritated. She only knew that he was. What had she done now?

"Stan was just leaving," she said. "Say good night, Stan."

"All right. I'll say it. But I won't mean it," Stan whispered provocatively. Reaching into his pocket to fish out a set of jangling car keys, he used one of the flat metal edges to suavely lift her chin—a rather dramatic action that made Joanna groan inside. His lips brushed hers again. "Have a good night, Joanna—if you can."

"I'll do my best," she promised, fighting the smile that was forming on her lips.

"Night, Simon."

Hearing Simon's answering grunt, Joanna opened the back door to let Stan out, then closed and locked it. Releasing a deep breath, she turned to Simon. "Party run late?"

"Do you care?"

Any urge to smile disappeared with the lift of her brows. "I'm interested."

"Considering that the guest of honor preferred an old movie, there didn't seem much point in making it a late evening."

"Oh. I hope no one left early on our account. But it was the last night of the festival and—"

"Ah, well, we can't let some snooty—I believe that's what you called it—faculty function stand in the way of a good time."

He was beginning to sound a lot like her mother. Joanna hated sarcastic condemnation, especially when she was the target. Being a slightly guilty target made it even worse. "Actually, it was a very nice reception. Everyone was friendly and polite."

"Too bad you and Stan didn't see fit to reciprocate."

"If you think we were rude, I'm sorry, but I doubt that anyone even noticed when we left."

"I did."

"Yes, well, don't let it keep you awake, Simon. I'm going to bed."

When he moved toward the table and she to her door, their paths intersected. She let him pass and then walked on.

"And then—kissing in the kitchen."

The accusation in his tone pulled her palm from the white wood of the door, brought her chin up slowly and put a helpless wry curve to her lips. He was jealous! At last a sign of human emotion. Joanna licked the reaction from her mouth and turned back to him. "Is there a rule against that?" she asked sweetly. "You should've told me."

His arms moved to a smooth crisscross of his chest, rising and falling evenly now. Joanna was treated to a view of long legs, crossed at the ankles, when he leaned against the table, its edge pressing into the backs of muscular thighs. "I heard giggling too," he mentioned.

"Oh, I get it." Joanna moved to his side, imitating his posture as she, too, leaned against the table. "No *giggling* during the kiss in the kitchen. Is that right?" When his eyes looked to the ceiling in disgust, she was quite pleased with her control of the situation. "I will kiss whomever I like, Simon."

He said nothing for a moment. Simon seemed deep in thought, no doubt plotting a snappy retort of some kind. She was unimpressed. Retorts invariably lost more snap the longer they went unspoken. Timing was all important.

But when his lips slowly curved to a knowing arc, her senses sharpened to mild alert. She blinked and waited, watching broad shoulders rise and shift toward her. The stare he aimed down at her was filled with such confidence, such dark intensity that her pleasure became edged with a new dimension . . . a sublime sense of anticipation. Her hips pressed harder against the tabletop.

"You're right, of course." The deep timbre of his

voice was soothing, at the same time unnerving. "But tell me, how did you like old *Octo*—"

"Fine." Joanna flushed beneath his hooded gaze.

"And yet you laughed."

"I don't expect every kiss to curl my toes," she clipped, placing both palms on the table behind her as an added support.

His voice took on a teasing quality. "I'll bet you wouldn't laugh if I kissed you."

She was sure of it. Simon's challenge brought a tingle that began at her nape and spread. She was treated to a rather disturbing demonstration of the trickle-down effect. He was now between her and the door. She probably ought to get out of this game. But her great curiosity —and her inability to move just yet—kept her there before him.

"Is that so?" she asked cockily, wishing the question hadn't come out so breathy. "Well, pucker up and give it a go. I'm game."

"Get your lips up here"—his eyes as well as his words mocked her—"I don't have my keys with me."

Oh, he was smug! She would laugh if it killed her. "Uh-uh. You'll have to come down here and get them. Bend a little, Simon." Surely he didn't expect *her* to put out the major effort in *his* operation.

He stepped very close, putting her at eye level with fawn-colored curls that peeked out from his open shirt. Joanna knew she would have to look up if she wanted to keep an eye on him. She thought it imperative. Besides, her cockiness would be nothing without a short lift of the chin, she rationalized.

Letting her head drop back, Joanna waited for his lips to descend. Even as the nonchalance remained in the set of her mouth, her eyes drank with interest the masculine features that had never before been this close to her. His nose was straight, flaring minutely at the tip. His eyebrows were much thicker than she had suspected at a distance. She wondered what it would be like to touch the rough-soft texture of his jaw. And those eyes . . . it was Nicky Newman all over again.

His hands went to her shoulders and lifted her to him, sweeping her palms from the table. The first touch of his lips on hers was tentative but very promising, softly persuasive. Nicky had never been that patient. She couldn't help but respond—passively, of course. Her fingers curled into itchy fists, restless with the temptation to skim along his ribs. Was that allowed? After all, this was only a test run.

But when his mouth began to move against hers in sensuous nudges, she let go of the reason and gave in to the lure of the manly chest within reach. Placing her palms against the crispness of his snug-fitting shirt, she began to feel and respond to the rhythm of slow and yet uneven breathing. When she pressed deeper into his warm body her insides tingled with a cool cascade of sensations, then drifted into pools of smoldering warmth.

Joanna slid her hands up and around his neck where her fingers savored the strength of his nape and the thick layers of soft hair there. He pulled her closer then and, without her palms between them, she could feel his chest taunting her breasts. His mouth glided over hers, stopping now and then to nip and suckle in the most intriguing way. The tip of his tongue teased until she began to chase it whimsically . . . slowly . . . in playful determination. Capturing it now and then between friendly lips, she tasted the sweetness and then released her hold to do it all again.

Simon made no fast moves that she could discern. At some point, which she couldn't remember, his hands had moved to her back, but what they did there was much more effective than anything Stan had done with all his roaming. Simon found virtually every pleasure point along her spine, giving each and every one special caressing attention before his fingers worked in a smooth swirling pattern to the sensitive patches just below her shoulder blades.

The heat in the room had increased. Or was it her own physical reaction that made the flesh beneath his collar sear the tips of her fingers? In any case, this was no game, she realized. This was serious business. She had no desire to laugh. She wanted to sigh with delight. And she did, but the sound came out broken and low, evidence of her tenuous control and the rapid cadence of her pulse. It was a condition that surprised her only because of its infrequency over the past few years. But when the feeling came she certainly knew what to do with it.

Without severing any of the intimate contact with him, she carefully stepped out of her pumps and moved even closer on the tips of her toes, letting them mingle in the pleasant company of his stockinged feet. His hands went to her hips, coaxing provocatively. She followed his direction, her thighs insinuating themselves against the hardness of his.

When she did that, a low groan issued from deep within him. He pulled back, releasing her lips to stare down from a lofty and somehow discomfiting angle. "Well?" he asked.

"You're no Nicky Newman," she said breathlessly, watching the labored movement of his throat as he swallowed.

"I see. Have you kissed him tonight too?" It was a dry question that came as Simon reached for her hands to remove them from around his neck. Aware of the slightest edge in his voice, and feeling slightly confused, she busied herself adjusting the waist of her dress. "Actually it was a long time ago."

"But memorable, obviously. Tell me, Joanna, will any pair of lips do?"

"What?" she asked, surprised by his attitude when she still savored the encounter.

"I mean, your mouth hardly had time to cool off from Stan."

Shaking her head, she then stared up at him in side-long disbelief. "Did I enjoy it a little more than you bargained for?"

He turned from her, lifting a hand to the back of his neck. "I have to admit that I didn't expect you to get quite so caught up in it."

"Well, excu-u-se me." Joanna swept her shoes from the floor, then rose to her full, indignant height. "As I recall, you weren't exactly an innocent bystander." He seemed irritated by his own enjoyment, making her suddenly irritated with hers. "It was a kiss, Simon—one that you wanted, by the way. I wanted it too. You were right. I didn't laugh. So what's the big deal?"

He turned on her, his jaw tight with restraint. "No big deal at all. But I don't understand you."

"What don't you understand?" Holding a shoe in each hand, Joanna rested the heels at either side of her waist.

"Well, my God, you're Richard's sister."

"So?" she demanded. "He and I came to grips with that *years* ago."

"Don't get snippety with me, Joanna. You know what I mean."

"No, I don't. Richard and I haven't interfered in each other's personal relationships since childhood. In any case, I hardly ever consult him about the simple matter of kissing. I'm funny that way," she added dryly and then flung an accusing glance. "You know what I think?" Without waiting for encouragement, she quickly continued, "I think that *you* think I'm trying to seduce you."

Offhand, he couldn't think of one single person who was better equipped for the job. "That's ridiculous. You wouldn't do that . . . would you?"

"What if I would?"

He cleared his throat. "Tell me more about your childhood."

"It isn't that interesting. I was chubby, spent two years with an orthodontist and, whenever anything upset me, I was known to walk in my sleep."

Oh, my God. On top of everything else, the woman walked in her sleep. "Do you—still do that?"

"Who knows?" she jeered with mock mystery, very real disgust for his attitude. "I've been living alone for the past several years. The neighbors have never complained, but you might want to lock your door just in case. After all, I might be dangerous. I could hang you up by your thumbs and have my way with you before you even knew it."

His glance was one of extreme forbearance. "Don't

you think you're a little short to make threats like that?"

"Maybe. Maybe not," she taunted. "Why, inside I might be a veritable hotbed of pent-up desires, untold passions, all screaming to get out." She pivoted, lifting a palm to shimmy in the air overhead as she sort of shuffled toward her part of the house. "Just watch out for Joanna, the short, but hot-blooded Hun . . ."

Simon watched for several moments the violent swing of the door until it gradually calmed to a lulling pendulum, finally ceasing all movement. Simultaneously feeling mild amusement and great frustration, he vigorously rubbed the strain of the past few minutes from his forehead. He'd never met anyone like her. And hoped to God he never would again. She was assertive, witty . . . and mad as hell at the moment. He hardly knew what to make of her. He'd spent the past several years with one woman, going through the various stages of courtship, marriage and divorce. Was this the new breed that had been in the making all the time he'd been out of circulation?

Simon didn't know. But suddenly he felt as though a good bit of time might have passed him by. Was he standing on the brink of something here? He didn't know that either. But he couldn't help wondering if he was up to finding out. She intrigued him. She challenged him. He might as well admit it. Joanna Sinclair stunned him.

Later, though, as he sank onto his recliner and leaned back, placing his hands behind his head to gaze at the ceiling, Simon ran it all through his mind once more. He'd done a stupid thing, kissing her like that. He should've saved the issue of the reception for a more opportune time. He should have stayed out of the kitchen altogether. At the very least, he should have gotten his glass of water—he wasn't even thirsty—and come straight back here to the living room to look over the next day's lecture. He should have done anything but what he *had* done. But God, her lips were there, primed and ready for him. And he'd been jealous—jealous! At his age! How juvenile could a grown man get. And then bringing Richard into it. Sheer idiocy.

There was something else, too, Simon realized. Something that had remained in the back of his mind ever since she'd said it. Something that brought an elusive tension to the hands that gripped the arms of the chair. What if she really did walk in her sleep . . . still. He chased away the vision, pronouncing it irrelevant, but the picture came again more vivid than before. What would happen if she came to his room late one night in her sleep? What if she slipped into bed beside him? What if she started to make love to him? What would he do?

There was a question of ethics here, he admitted, shifting uncomfortably. Would he wake her up and send her back to her own bed? Or would he pretend he had no idea she was asleep? Maybe. Maybe not. Letting his head drop back to the leather, he closed his eyes against the faint lamplight and spent quite a long time perusing the possibilities.

Soon the principle became lost in a myriad of tantalizing scenarios, and Simon very much wished to be tested on the question.

CHAPTER FOUR

Joanna sensed by some inner clock that she was sleeping late, defying time and all its demands. At dawn she'd instinctively begun to relish each and every delicious moment. Lulled by a Saturday morning serenade of birds outside the shaded window, she curled herself up and let the gentle movement of the water bed rock her into oblivion. Her lips curved with the sheer heaven of it all.

At first the noise was a hum, low and insignificant. She rolled over to snuggle deeper into the bedclothes. The sound came closer, rumbling like the rapid puttputt of a go-cart through her drowsiness. Go away, she ordered irritably. Then a full-throttle roar reached her ears, stiffening every muscle. The backfire shot her right out of the bed. Flinging the covers, she twisted the face of the clock and squinted. Turning it from her sight, she moaned. Seven A.M. *Seven!* God, she would get him for this.

Joanna swept the window curtain aside and struggled to raise the sash. She couldn't see him, but she knew it had to be Simon. Who else would mow a stupid lawn at this hour? When he came into view at the side of the house, she drew a bolstering breath to compete with the now thunderous din.

"Hey! Hey, you!"

He didn't hear her. Simon went right on, staring intently at the ground as he mowed effortlessly past her window. The man was demented.

"*Si*-mon! Simon—damn you—stop that noise!"

But he never looked up from beneath the jaunty panama hat he wore with a knit shirt and cotton twill shorts.

"I'll kill him."

With a punctuating sigh Joanna lowered the window. Her shoulders sagged with lingering fatigue, but she managed a grumpy kick at the fallen blanket by her bed. She'd been cozy—so cozy—beneath the covers. Her sleeveless nightie offered little comfort in the cool room. Her body felt heavy as she dragged herself into the bathroom to wash. The action slowly widened her eyes by degrees until she had gathered enough energy to dress in a tee shirt and cutoffs. Shoes could damn well wait until she'd had her coffee. As Joanna made her way into the kitchen, she met with further frustration.

Damn. She was out of coffee. A groan accompanied her to the refrigerator, where she settled for a soft drink. Taking sweet vengeance in tossing the tab top onto the counter—and leaving it there—she stepped out into the morning sunlight on the patio. Cooled by a soft breeze, the uneven stone teased her toes and her disposition as she moved to a chaise longue and flopped herself onto the cushions. A sip of her drink tingled her throat and made her shiver. She set the chilled can on a nearby table and took a surly look around her.

Dew still clung like a glaze of cut diamonds to the unmown grass in the backyard. She hoped the blade of Simon's lawn mower would rust. Her El Camino sat beside his station wagon in the driveway. She hoped flying rocks would pelt his fender when he showed up here to mow.

Joanna closed her eyes and sat for several minutes, allowing the sun to gradually warm her lips to a tolerant curve. It wasn't so bad on the patio, she guessed. Given the chance, she could go to sleep right here. Simon had apparently moved to the other side of the house. The noise was now a far-off drone. But when a gust of wind feathered brown strands of hair across her face, Joanna lifted her lashes again. Obviously she couldn't sleep here.

Pushing herself up from the chaise, she strolled past the late-summer flowers that bordered the patio. Drawn by a childhood memory, she bent down beside an ornate birdbath to pluck a fuzzy dandelion—one of the few weeds in the yard, she noted—and carried it back to her seat, twirling the stem between thumb and forefinger as she went. Once Richard would have fought her for the heady pleasure of blowing on a dandelion. But he wasn't here. Today she had it all to herself.

Blowing directly on to the ball-shaped flower, she watched the filaments float out on the breeze. It took two long breaths to strip the core of all the fibers. When it was done, Joanna wondered lazily if she should get another dandelion and do it again. Yes, she thought she might. But she didn't get up right away.

Sounds from the engine crescendoed and she looked up in time to see Simon coming around the corner of the house. A hint of a sheen covered his face and arms, giving the slightest glow to his tan. She found it oddly irritating that the muscles of his thighs hardly strained as he pushed the mower.

Spotting her, he smiled his surprise, tipping his hat as he purposefully mowed past her chair and right over the coveted cluster of dandelions. The only cluster.

Disgust brought Joanna struggling to her feet. An unconscionable streak of anger shot through her at seeing the only pleasure she had known that morning chopped to smithereens.

"Bastard," she muttered, slamming the door as she entered the kitchen.

Fingers wrapping the handle loosely, Simon swung the mower around, heading for the patio again. Now you see her, now you don't, he mused, wondering why she'd suddenly vacated such a cozy spot. Anyway, he was glad to see her up and around after that nonsense about sleeping late. It could only make her a better person, he thought with a slow smile. He'd heard no complaints about her teaching either, although he wasn't about to endorse her methods.

Filling his nostrils with the sweet smell of newly mown grass, Simon continued his pattern of straight rows, neat thoughts. Perhaps he was having some small influence on Joanna. Maybe she was adjusting. It had been that way with him and Susan too. There were many adjustments before things worked out for them.

Simon frowned at his mistake. Things *hadn't* worked out, he reminded himself wryly. He remembered clearly the consensus that things hadn't worked out at all. Hell, he had been too set in his ways in the first place to be good at marriage. He was lucky Susan hadn't ended up hating him. He needed solitude—much more than marriage offered. Still, he missed the nicer moments with the opposite sex. But the moments always seemed to turn into expectations, commitment that he couldn't give. No, a lifetime was just too much.

Forever? Simon shook his head. Never again.

But Joanna, well . . .

Thoughts of her smile returned like a slowly rising tide, licking provocatively at his reason. He was attracted. Even if she didn't do things exactly his way. Maybe she would want to go with him today. He had everything planned to his satisfaction. It couldn't hurt to ask.

Simon's feet began to move a little faster. He finished the lawn in record time and restored the mower and his panama hat to their usual places in the shipshape garage. As he crossed the patio, the sight of a nearly full can of soda put a frown on his forehead, a sigh on his lips. How could she drink this stuff first thing in the morning?

As he entered the kitchen, the slam of a cabinet door greeted Simon. Swallowing his mild irritation, he took the soda to the sink and began to pour.

"Don't do that." Joanna was beside him, snatching the can from his grasp. "That's mine."

"But it's hot, Joanna, and—"

"*Just* the way I like it," she snapped, and then softened at the waspish sound of her voice. "Anyway, I don't have any coffee. Do you—have any coffee?"

"I usually keep instant for guests, but—"

"That would do."

74

"—I'm out." Simon took a glass from the dishwasher and turned the tap. "Water is always good."

She eyed the clear liquid suspiciously. "Water is for taking aspirin and bathing. Besides, this pop will hit the spot." She took a demonstrative swig and tried not to cough at the lukewarm, acid taste. "Great," she rasped, her eyes watering slightly from the sting in her throat.

Simon shook his head in dismal comment. "Anything to get your daily dose of caffeine. What about breakfast?"

"Never touch it. Breakfast foods don't feel right in my mouth."

"My God," he breathed. "Are you from earth?" Seeing the offended lift of her finely shaped brow, Simon turned away, ordering his concern for her personal habits to cease. It was, after all, none of his business— although she badly needed to be taken in tow. "Never mind." He paused with the need to put the question in the right way. "Have any special plans for today?"

"Oh, yes," she assured, the memory of day's awakening returning full force. "I'll be taking a nap as soon as possible. A long one."

Simon kept his face straight as he turned back to her. The muscles were beginning to ache from all the expressions she'd put there. "But you just got up."

"Not my idea, believe me. After my nap, I may go for a walk."

"Well, I have some plans. Would you like to come with me to an auction?"

"What? No more sunrise lawn care?" she asked dryly. "Maybe you'd like to get out the file and blunt all the thorns on the roses or something."

Joanna went into mild shock at the light poke and the

linger of a masculine fingertip at the hollow between her breasts. Her blue eyes focused, unwavering, on the emerald sting in his. His hot breath warmed her cheeks.

"Look, *you.*" His voice was cool, smooth and she thought she should pay attention. "I'm trying to get along with you. Believe me, it isn't easy. Don't get sarcastic just because I like a neat lawn. Now I've just extended a polite invitation. Be kind enough to answer in that vein." Simon lowered his hand slowly to his side.

"O-kay." She let the lilt in each syllable mislead. "I'd love to go with you, Simon." Despite her anger, it was one of the more encouraging moves he'd made. Besides, she'd never been to an auction. "But I think you should understand one thing," she said silkily, lifting a feminine finger to that part of his chest exposed by the open placket of his shirt. "Don't ever again touch me *there*" —sliding down with gentle swirls, she teased the feathery hair—"unless you mean business." Joanna finished with a curt poke to his breastbone before giving up the intimate contact.

Simon stared for a long moment at the subtle challenge in her eyes. He was amused. He was confused. He was excited too, but looked away before that last emotion could gain a firm foothold. A decided smile touched his lips as he mentally shook his head in temporary resignation. He couldn't nag her. He couldn't bully her. He wondered if he could love her. The thought dangled somewhere in his consciousness as he walked to his door.

"Give me twenty minutes," he said.

Joanna took forty-five and made them late.

She spent the entire day with Simon. It wasn't long before she realized that when the man said he had plans, he . . . had . . . plans. He didn't take her to one auction. He took her to three, scheduled at odd hours throughout the day. Parking the car a few blocks from the first sale, he shooed her across the street toward a long, low building.

Refusing to be rushed on a Saturday, she retrieved her elbow from his grasp—"If you don't mind"—and dashed into an ice-cream parlor for two dips of fudge ripple to go. When she lagged behind on the sidewalk, licking the dip that teetered precariously atop a sugar cone, Simon came back to clutch at her elbow again—more firmly this time.

At the auction she bid on an old butter churn which Simon summarily denounced as "not worth your money." He seemed so sure, staring straight ahead, his attractive jaw poised in unquestionable knowledge, that Joanna stayed with the bidding and afterward asked him to tote the wooden crock to the car. He obliged grudgingly, still muttering, *"Definitely* not worth your money."

She loved it! And despite his cautious smiles, his occasional grumpiness at having his schedule "shattered," she thought he rather liked having her around too. Celebrating her enjoyment of the day and her companion, Joanna licked the hot mustard on a corn dog as he drove them to the second event on the other side of town.

This time, Simon came away with a battered cherrywood dresser that he immediately dubbed "perfect for an upstairs bedroom and good as new when it's refinished." As she helped him lift the cumbersome piece into the back of the station wagon, Joanna thought his expectations remarkably high. By then she was an old hand at auctions and couldn't help shaking her head in disagreement. "Definitely not worth your time."

When he stopped at a small restaurant, nestled in Springfield's hilly countryside, she pronounced herself "stuffed" and declined his offer of a late lunch. Simon directed her to a chair opposite him while he showed her "a civilized meal" and told her she had some nerve calling herself a consumer advocate. She assured him she had plenty of nerve. Thoroughly amused, Joanna made a point of complimenting his balanced selection from the four basic food groups.

It was early evening before Simon pointed the car in the direction of home. On the way back to the city, Joanna, pleasantly tired and hungry again, curled up to relax on the seat beside him. For the first time, she'd had fun with Simon. She treasured it all the more because it was the unexpected kind of fun that occurred with spontaneity, impulse. Not like "programmed" good times, she thought, fully aware that he might argue the point.

When Simon paused at an intersection on the outskirts of Springfield, she stared languidly at the flashing neon of a Taco Bill sign. Before she could speak, he was pulling into the parking lot. "One, with everything?" he asked resignedly.

Suddenly hesitant, Joanna dipped her chin rather shyly. "Might as well make it two."

"Now, Simon I know we can work this out."

"Tell me how, Joanna." Sleeves rolled to the elbow, he leaned over the sink, peeling potatoes fiercely. "I've got people coming tonight. You've got a different set of people coming. And there's a tub of cole slaw in my

78

refrigerator where I planned to marinate my sole."
Pointing the peeler, Simon looked meaningfully at
Joanna. "Now, I think that pretty well puts the situa-
tion in the proper perspective."

Failing to see just *how* it did that, she nevertheless
humored him—a little. "It's hardly a tub," she countered, "but I'll move my slaw to make room for your
fish. Anything else?"

"Oh, yes. There's a lot more," he assured, resuming
the job at hand. "You've cluttered my kitchen with paper bags. They're everywhere I turn, filled with God
knows what. Your ice chest is right in front of the cabinet and—"

Joanna took hold of the metal handle and began pulling the chest out of his way. "Say no more—Simon
Legree," she murmured.

"I heard that," he accused. "All this could've been
avoided if you'd only told me you were planning to ask
your students here—tonight."

She knew it would be useless to remind him that she
had told him on Wednesday that she'd invited her students for Friday and that he'd been stewing ever since,
although they hadn't discussed it again—until now. Simon was obviously a little nervous about his dinner
party for a few members of the faculty—a dinner to
which she'd been invited—on Wednesday—but had by
necessity declined. Their signals had crossed. She re-
gretted that, but didn't see any great catastrophe in it.
She and her guests would be out on the patio, far away
from him and his precious sit-down dinner.

Leaving the ice chest at the back door, Joanna went
to his side. "Anything I can do to help?"

"No," he muttered. "You have your own preparations to make."

"Most everything's done." Pushing aside a platter of barbecued ribs and two different brands of sauce to make room for her hips, Joanna lifted herself onto the counter top. "The baked beans are warming in the microwave. The music's ready and waiting on the patio. No use setting the table until someone gets here to hold the plates down—the wind, you know. For now, I'm free as a bird."

"Yes, well, I suppose it isn't difficult when you leave it all to Dixie Cup and the Quik Trip Deli. It must be great to work right out of a brown paper bag."

Refusing to succumb to his grumpiness, Joanna lifted her chin to aid a smug smile. "As you can see, Simon, I am unabashed. They're not coming to check out my culinary talents or my selection in china."

"Coming to trade albums and tapes, are they?"

"Whoa! Aren't *we* the temperamental chef tonight."

"Yes, I guess we are," he said coolly, and seemed proud of the disposition as he lifted the collander of potatoes from the sink. "Now, get off my counter so I can slice these."

Joanna did as he ordered, but not without a glance of pretended offense over one shoulder. Transferring the heavy carton of slaw to a lower shelf in the refrigerator, she then took a seat at the kitchen table, turning her chair to give herself a good view of him.

As she watched Simon work, Joanna thought his profile quite handsome, if not for the slightest scowl on his face. And even that didn't lower her appraisal very much. The appealing stretch of navy knit across his back and shoulders more than made up for bad moods that usually passed quickly, she had discovered. And she ought to know. She was adept at bringing them on with no trouble at all.

His bibbed apron was a no-nonsense beige oilcloth. But the way it gaped at the back and exposed an attractive patch of camel-colored trouser, outlining quite nicely the muscles in his hips, well . . . the man obviously knew good tailoring and had the body to do it justice. It was a body she had begun to watch more and more, despite—or who could tell? maybe *because* of—Simon's reluctance to let her see too much of it. In more ways than one.

"Hmph."

Her unintentional murmur brought Simon's head around in seeming apathy. "Did you say something?"

Joanna met his gaze with as much innocence as she could muster. "No."

Waiting until he returned to his slicing, she stretched her legs out to the floor and tapped the table restlessly. This mix-up in plans couldn't have come at a worse time, she thought. After their Saturday outing, Simon had begun to loosen up a little. At least he seemed more tolerant. Twice since then, he had even sought her company. On Sunday afternoon, after she'd slept twelve hours straight and loved every minute of it, he'd come out to sit with her on the patio. The talk had been of Richard mostly and the book they had co-authored. But she'd enjoyed it, somehow relieved to know that at times he, too, was lonely.

With a silent, slow sigh, Joanna remembered Tuesday. She'd been doing laundry when he'd wandered into the kitchen and struck up a lively debate on current economic trends and their potential for "absolute chaos." It was a subject that both had warmed to. She had also found herself warming to him—for all the good it had done. Simon seemed to possess an uncanny ability for concentration on the subject at hand, a restrained intensity in whatever he set his mind to. She admired that, but . . .

Simon placed a layer of neatly sliced potatoes into a casserole and then lifted a finger to the page of a propped-up cookbook. As she watched his intent scan of a recipe, Joanna couldn't help wishing that she could be the target of all that single-minded concentration, that she could have all that leashed intensity unleashed on her sometime. Her brows lifted instinctively at the exciting prospect. What would he do if she stepped right up to him and whipped off his oil-cloth apron? What would he do if she slammed his book shut and kissed him in a way that he couldn't refuse? Her thoughts began to blossom, matching a burgeoning pulse. She cleared her throat of a sudden constriction.

His sidelong glance evolved to a questioning stare. "What *is* it, Joanna?"

"Nothing." Impatient with his impatience and his tone, she drew herself up from the chair and walked to the back door, her hand on the knob before she spoke again. "At least nothing that you deserve to know."

Oh, he would get her.

Ignoring the cluttered remains of Joanna's barbecue, Simon stood at the sink, his teeth clenching a little more with each dish he rinsed before loading them into the dishwasher. He didn't usually go to such trouble—my God, he wasn't *that* meticulous—but it gave him something to do with his hands, hands that itched to encircle that treasonous little neck of hers. It had to be the worst evening he'd ever spent as a host. It even topped last year's faculty follies in humiliation. And it was all her fault. Simon couldn't wait until her last guest had gone. Then, by God, he would get her.

Oblivious to the clatter of plate against stainless steel, but very conscious of the low conversation and intermittent laughter *still* coming from the patio, Simon went over each transgression and the guilty parties involved.

From the very beginning, his dinner had bombed, starting with Mimi Hampton's vow that she couldn't wait to get at "that great-smelling barbecue." And then there was Gina—whom he hadn't even planned to invite before Joanna's decline. When Gina had sworn that the Little River Band, fairly blasting from the patio, left her "absolutely limp with passion," well . . . he hadn't said it, but his heretofore unbiased opinion of cosmetology had lowered considerably. His Englebert Humperdink never had a chance.

Stan's offense was the worst, though. In the midst of the conversation on the very real plight of teachers' salaries, Stan had suddenly burst out laughing, obviously in response to the punch line of a joke being told outside. Joanna's story *had* been amusing—what little of it Simon could catch—but it hardly deserved Stan's tears, for God's sake.

Simon supposed that at one time or another, every guest in his dining room had looked wistfully toward that patio. He'd been tempted—so tempted—to tell them all to get the hell outside and join the heathens. And Joanna had been right in the middle of the orgy. He could see her now, bare feet tucked beneath her, laughing, enjoying, smacking her greasy lips in delight. Probably licking her fingers too.

His groan was low and begrudging. He refused to think anymore about the admittedly sensual vision of her doing all that. The noise had dwindled now to Joanna's throaty feminine hum. Drying his hands on a dish towel, Simon moved toward the window, weighing his chances of being discovered should he part the curtain slightly and look out. But then the door opened and he turned quickly away.

Holding an empty platter, Joanna closed the door with a self-congratulatory onside kick, then sighed her success of the evening. "Hi, Simon. How'd it go?"

"Need you ask?"

Ignoring the warning tone and his ramrod spine, she set the platter on the counter and lifted soothing fingers to knead the strain in her shoulders. "Umm. That feels good."

"Wipe your mouth."

"What?"

He dropped the dish towel onto the counter and then nodded toward it before moving to the table. "Your mouth. Wipe it."

Piqued by his curt demand and her own fatigue, she nevertheless complied, not with the towel, but with an exaggerated sweep of her forearm. Joanna watched with mild pleasure the disgusted shake of his head. "Look, Simon, it's been a long evening—"

"You'll never know how long, Joanna."

"—so if you've got something to say, just spit it out so I can clean up and relax."

"Spit it out?" he asked coolly. "You want me to spit it out? All right—" He came to stand very close, so close

84

that she was forced to lean, tilting her head backward to get a good look at the green anger in his eyes. "You're insensitive and you ruined my dinner. How's that for openers?"

"Oh, come on, Simon, let's get real," she said, warily stepping out of the line of fire. "I wasn't even at your dinner."

"The fact that you did it from a distance makes it even worse. You were rude, Joanna. You and your guests were loud and rude and had no consideration for the rest of us. And what about my neighbors? My God, the Wilsons next door are elderly. They need their rest. But I knew it would be this way. You could've post- poned your barbecue for another time, but no, in all your insensitivity, you insisted on having the students here tonight. And I'm mad as hell about it."

The steady stream of accusations brought Joanna's chin up by angry degrees as she faced him. "That isn't true, Simon. You're mad as hell because I had them here at all. You disapproved of the whole idea. And as for the Wilsons, they damned sure looked wide awake to me when they wandered onto the patio. The last to leave, in fact. And if you call me insensitive one more time, I'll drop-kick you from here to the moon, buster."

The evening had been a strain for her too. But she'd made the most of it. She would've preferred to be with him—on the patio, in his dining room. Wherever. But no. It hadn't worked out. She had considered canceling her plans—now *that* would've been rude. He could've suggested that both groups pool their resources and have dinner together. But no. He hadn't done that. That would've required flexibility. That would've required impulse, spontaneity—and a desire to be with her. She was dealing with a man who didn't know the meaning of those words. But if he expected an apology, he could damn well wait until his day lilies sprouted wings and flew. "Simon, you know what your problem is?"

His mouth opened in wonder. "I thought I just told you my problem. It's you. While you were out there having your fun, you never once con—"

"That's it, isn't it?" she said with several short, knowing nods. "We had fun and you didn't. Well"—Joanna threw up her hands—"I'll remember that from here on out. No fun unless Simon is included."

"Come off it, Joanna—"

"—and I'll tell you something else," she said hotly. "You could enjoy yourself a lot more if you weren't such a . . . such a stick in the mud. I hate to say this, but sometimes you're as dull as dishwater, you know that?" There was a look of utter shock on his face. But Joanna would say it all, insulting him as he had insulted her. "You're a dinosaur, Simon. Extinct, with a capital E. And I—and I . . . have nothing more to say on the subject."

Joanna left the room in a huff, letting the door swing wide as she did so. Already a tinge of regret was picking at her conscience but she ignored it, preferring to focus on her anger at the moment. He had some nerve. Some nerve, she thought, marching into the bathroom to strip off her clothes and pin up her hair. She turned on the shower, adjusting the heat and flow before stepping inside to let the warm water pelt her pulse back to a less agitated state.

She didn't want to think about what had happened. Nevertheless, the memory throbbed, relentless, as she soaped herself heartlessly. She hadn't been prepared for his ambush. Well, next time she would be ready. She would be cool. She would be armed to the teeth next time. He'd called her insensitive. For that, he deserved everything she had said. She wasn't insensitive—not to him. She was aware of Simon at all times. Whenever he frowned. Whenever he smiled—infrequently, maybe, but God, when he did it was nice.

Turning off the tap, she dried herself roughly, knowing she'd get nowhere with those thoughts. Her feelings had been frustrated at every turn. Struggling into a white terry-cloth robe, she tied the belt securely. He did everything by the book. *His* book. And so far, she could see no chapter for her, which annoyed her. He *was* inflexible, she assured herself. He *was* compulsive. He didn't have an impromptu bone in his body.

But as Joanna made her way back to the dining room and pushed open the door, remembering the grim line of his mouth, she knew that she had lied. He wasn't dull —or a dinosaur. She could never be so attracted to a dull dinosaur. And she was attracted. That was the problem.

A brief scan of the kitchen brought more regret. Simon wasn't there, but the room was spotless, everything put away. He'd cleaned up her mess too. She doubted she'd have done that for him. But she was touched that he—despite his anger—had done it for her.

Joanna moved to his door and, without knocking, entered, knowing she was about to do something she rarely did. Apologize. The infrequency of such action weighted her body, slowing her feet some, but she pushed herself past the darkened dining area and into his living room.

A masculine murmur turned her face to the shadowy

form that was Simon. Hands thrust into trouser pockets, he was pacing an angry path between the sofa and the bar and back again. "I'm not dull," he muttered tightly. "By God, I'm not extinct either. I can be as impulsive as the next person—when I have to be."

As though in resolve to prove it, his knuckles rapped the bar top once before he suddenly veered from his path and moved toward a table by the wall. When he reached for an expensive-looking vase and held it in one huge palm, Joanna forced back her frown of confusion and waited.

In the soft glow of moonlight spilling through the window, Simon seemed to weigh the different options. For a long and thoughtful minute his hard expression vacillated between stark determination and nagging doubt. Still Joanna didn't move, her own mind filled with conflicting emotions as to what he should do . . . what he *would* do . . . what she would have already done in a situation like this.

But Simon was nothing like Joanna. She knew that. And so she was not surprised when finally his shoulders sagged slightly and he sighed in resignation.

It was then that he noticed her presence. He stiffened once more, looking everywhere but where she was, obviously a bit dismayed with having an audience for his self-scrutiny. But gradually relaxing again, he turned confessing eyes to her and shrugged. "I can't do it, Joanna."

It was a softly crooned admission, holding neither telltale guilt nor smugness. A mere statement of fact. One that constricted her throat and drained her frustration, filling her eyes, her chest, with tender affection.

"Does that surprise you?" Joanna went forward, to

take the fragile vase from his grasp before he changed his mind.

"No, not really." He turned away and went to the sofa, which gave beneath the weight of both his body and his mood. "It's rather in keeping with my image, I suppose. I'm a complete stranger to impulse."

Not knowing quite how to respond, she sighed her own sense of responsibility, guilt and the wry wonder that she even felt that way. "I was wrong, Simon. I shouldn't have said you were . . . I shouldn't have said those things. Because they're not true." She put the vase back on the table and moved to sit on the sofa, turning her body toward Simon. Her knees drawn to rest on the cushion, she adjusted the hem of her robe to cover her thighs. "As for being a stranger to impulse . . . well, you might be more lucky than you know. I, being well acquainted with it, sometimes say things, unfair things, when I'm angry . . . or tired. . . ."

She ignored his preoccupied nod of agreement.

"I guess I was intolerant," he offered grimly.

"That's all right." Her hand went with the instinct to soothe, lifting to touch and then caress the masculine arm that rested along the back of the sofa. "You couldn't help it."

Beneath a most patient sidelong glance that evolved very slowly into a smile, Joanna felt her own tension subside, a more heady feeling flowing back in its place. She drew a deep yet fragmented breath of his tantalizing scent. His arm and the fine hair that covered it teased her fingertips to sensitive pads of seduction, but she didn't look in that direction. She was watching him watch her, his eyes filled with a new and revealing emerald awareness.

"Truce?" he asked, turning his chest toward her.

She lifted her brows in agreement. She was afraid to move anything else. Afraid that any distraction might make him look away. "I can live with that."

Joanna had come to think she could live with lots of things. She could live nicely with the dusky masculine appreciation in his eyes. It blended sensually with her own long and unrequited attraction to him. She could live nicely with the delicious nearness of him. Kiss me, Simon, she breathed cautiously, and yet her lungs felt strangely reckless. Kiss me now and mean it.

Her tongue wanted badly to wet her slightly parted lips in anticipation. Its tip lingered just inside one corner of her mouth, waiting. Her fingers had stopped the gentle movement along his forearm. They too waited, craving, demanding, further incentive from Simon.

When a masculine palm spanned the distance to caress her nape, all time seemed to cease for Joanna. The moment stood still as he pulled her to him, lowering his mouth to set her lips tingling, her mind reeling in a slow spiral of a new and different confrontation. It was all she had hoped it would be, his tongue gliding, outlining her lips with erotic intent. She lifted a palm to his cheek as encouragement.

With tender nudges that radiated desire, he gradually molded his mouth to hers. Her fingers moved upward past a pulsating temple to luxuriate in the toasty softness of his hair. Hair that she had known would be thick and inviting. He held her to him, his hand now playing along the intricate length of her spine, coaxing, urging the intimate contact.

Sliding her knees from their bent position, Joanna leaned into him, a bare thread of restraint warning her to move slowly, think about what she was doing, although she wanted desperately not to think. She wanted to feel. But when her breasts brushed his chest and then lingered, heat singing through terry cloth, an involuntary moan of delight escaped her.

Slowly, Simon pulled his lips from hers, his green eyes blazing a question narrowed by caution. She returned his stare, hoping that he would come back to her again, entreating him with trembling lips. His hesitation gave way to an undeniable desire for another taste of her mouth. He was hers for another few seconds, their tongues mingling in bold pursuit and retreat before he sighed the frustration of his own restraint. But he didn't let go completely.

He kept her in the circle of his arms, settling her against the hardness of his chest . . . the chest that had for weeks teased her hands to touch it. She did that now, savoring for long moments the feel of Simon's warmth, the rapid cadence of his heart. Closing her eyes, she let her head nestle sweetly in the cradle of his neck. A manly thigh caressed her feminine one, half exposed now by the slight gape of her robe. His hand moved to that place, sending flutters of hot temptation through her. The excruciating lightness of his touch seared the sensitive skin. Her heart began to tap an earthy and urgent rhythm. The time had come to decide. She wanted him. But was now the right time? For her? For him?

She knew by the sudden clinching of his fist that Simon was about to make that decision for her. When he hovered a split second over her robe before closing the slit to pat the material and the alluring flesh beneath, Joanna knew she had lost him to reason. And even though she swam in her own doubts, her heart, her lips began immediately to mourn the loss in miserable silence.

He moved from her side and stood, clearing his throat for what she knew would be a tender, but oh so reasonable, explanation. One that she really didn't want or need to hear, mainly because she wasn't the first one to think of it.

His voice was a husky rasp. "Joanna, we need to think about what we could be starting here." His hands went into his pockets now. Warmed by the reminder of where they had been only a few moments before, she was already beginning to regret his decision.

"You're right, of course," she said breathily. Standing to adjust her robe, Joanna smiled a bittersweet smile. "We're very different people, Simon. I don't suppose it would do to let our . . . attraction get—" She lifted her gaze to his. "It is okay to admit I'm attracted, isn't it?"

He smiled a tender, reluctant agreement, but the line of his jaw was unyielding. "I think we've both pretty well established our feelings on that. But you know where it would've led—"

"Oh, listen," she brushed past him, sending a backhanded wave of dismissal, "say no more. I'm sure it would've been awful—" Joanna stopped and turned back. "Not awful," she amended. "I didn't mean that. I'm sure it would've been wonder—" Her shoulders sagged with ragged frustration. "Good night, Simon."

CHAPTER FIVE

Sometime around two o'clock in the morning, he became a regular person.

The transformation was slow, but Joanna tossed and turned until, in wistful dreams, she made it happen, directing the scene through a gossamer twilight sleep. She saw herself resting innocently on the patio. It was evening. Stars had just begun to twinkle in a velvet sky when Simon approached. And there on the chaise longue, he magically became like her, casual, easygoing. He sneered in the face of convention. And when she inquired about his plans for the following day, he hardly knew what he'd be doing for the next five minutes. The confession was a thoroughly seductive one.

She'd been wrong. Simon assured her that he liked fudge ripple ice cream. He loved water beds. He *adored* her. And no amount of reason or protest would convince him otherwise. Oh, she tried her best to distract him. But he wouldn't listen, his passion too strong, too intense to be denied. At last he was hers. Anything that didn't fit the fantasy was erased with an ease found only in dreams. She charmed him unmercifully, spinning silken threads of laughter through his soul.

Simon swept her into his arms and kissed her without doubts, without reservations, without worry of where it would lead. They both knew and embraced the exciting certainty. With tender growls and luscious nibbles, he made love to her. Joanna, Joanna, he crooned over and over again as she spun slowly, surely, deliciously in his arms.

At the point of total surrender, total ecstasy, her eyes fluttered maddeningly to groggy alert, her heart still pounding with the thrill of it all, the frustration of it all. As she lay in the darkness, alone again, the only thought in her head was to make the dream reality. Her body, her mind, ached for that ultimate experience.

In a split second of decision, she put her feet to the floor and moved in his direction, determined—driven. No more nonsense about differences. The most important element now was what they shared. Desire. He wanted her. She wanted him. And nothing should stand in the way of that. She would see that it didn't—now.

The air in the kitchen was cool against her bare stomach and breasts, but Joanna was seized by a warmth, a desire that permeated her being. Moving through the house, she felt buoyant and secure in her mission. At the darkened doorway of his bedroom, his words stopped her, but not for long.

"Joanna . . . is that you?" His voice was raspy and deep, as though he had known she would come.

"It's me," she whispered, following the sound of the long low breath he expelled, all the time hoping he wouldn't demand an explanation. She was unable to utter one. But given the chance, she could show him.

Slipping beneath the cool covers, Joanna aligned her body along the warm length of his, the intimate contact stealing her own breath momentarily. He lay on his back, his unexpected nudity inciting her already tingling nerves to riot. She braced herself on a trembling elbow and reached for him, feeling her way past a muscled arm to palm a pounding chest and entangle her fingers in the feathery hair there.

She moved over his chest and then let a fingertip trace the line of his collarbone, memorizing the texture, the rugged terrain of the man beside her. Her finger zipped a slow and taunting path down the center of him to his navel, which she circled provocatively and entered teasingly before moving on to a most titillating forest below.

There she discovered and wooed the undeniable evidence of his desire. With light strokes she encouraged, leaning over to kiss his lips tentatively. But the effect on her own mouth was irrefutably certain and she found herself lingering there to let her tongue convey a heartfelt entreaty. He responded, not with a demand for explanation, but with a deep, determined groan.

He shifted, pushing her onto her back to begin his own devastating seduction. She knew at once he would not be complacent or passive. A hot, sweet love blew over her eyes to close them in time for the onslaught. Fiery kisses, slow and moist, branded her throat, her cheeks, then went to her mouth in sultry, succulent movements. He lay half on, half off her flat stomach. Long masculine fingers climbed her ribs to cup one of her breasts tenderly.

She stretched her arms outward in consent, feeling much like a sexy goddess awaiting royal attention. She relished the feel of his tongue moving over a nipple in sensual adoration, his hand stroking, searing, caressing. With a husky sigh, Joanna offered up herself in primeval sacrifice.

Then, as though he thought her too smug for her own good, Simon slid a muscular thigh between her legs in firm reminder that she was, after all, human with a very basic human need. Her arms curled around his back to hold him. She didn't forget again, for he didn't let her.

From that point on, she was caught up in the scents, the sounds and sensations of love, which took on new and heightened dimensions. It was he that made it so. And she responded in a way that she had never before experienced, knowing, despite all her earlier dreaming, she'd been unprepared for *this* Simon.

Where she had meant to lead, he took complete control. Where she had meant to coax, he made undeniable demands. And what she had envisioned as a languorous dreamlike affair, he transformed to a fiery passionate siege with sure possession of her as his aim.

He incited a raging storm within her. His kisses left her weak and breathless, yet aching for more. She was swept into his erotic realm of delight, consumed by his one-man conspiracy. And all the time she stayed with him, encouraging that most wicked, delicious campaign, her hands caressing, rewarding, suggesting.

His tongue circled down the middle of her rib cage, flicking fire to the flesh in its path. She was drawn into a mindless fury, drugged by the elemental fierceness of his need. He knew when to linger and when to retreat. She clung to him, lost in the foray he inspired, her muscles alert with anticipation, a tinge of apprehension, yet wanting him all the same.

When he moved onto her, she held him, guiding him into her moist, welcoming warmth. His strokes were feather-light at first, making her squirm in the earthy scintillation. Then he advanced with deep and glorious plunges. All the time his hands, his lips teased, driving her to greater heights until she wanted to scream her feverish need to be taken.

At that moment when she thought she *would* scream, he knew and shared her dilemma. Catching her hips in his hands, he began a taunting and steady rhythm that crescendoed moment by moment, taking her with him on a spiraling path right up to what seemed the very edge of eternity.

In desperation, she stepped into a rampaging sea and precious release. Simon caught his breath, clinging to one last thread of control until an arching thrust of her hips dragged him over the edge with her, unleashing the storm within him. It raged for several seconds, until finally he collapsed in her embrace.

She lay in silence for long, floating moments, letting her comfort surround him, letting his warmth engulf her. And when she could think again, Joanna knew that any questions, any doubts she'd had about Simon as a lover had been irrevocably—delectably—laid to rest. He'd come through with guns blazing, she thought, her mind still reeling with the memory. She hadn't even suspected he possessed such fire, such tenderness, such command, but now she knew and the knowledge licked through her veins.

Had it really happened? Her smile was slow and lilt-ing. Indeed, it had, with more excitement than she'd ever imagined. And she had imagined a lot.

Simon shifted to rest at her side, his arm now lazily draping her breasts. "Joanna?"

"Hmmm?" The sound was a husky purr from deep within her throat.

"Tell me something," he whispered. "Are you . . . are you awake?"

"Mmmm. It feels more like a dream . . . a wonderful dream."

She felt him stiffen beside her. "Aw, Christ," he murmured. His sigh seemed more of a groan. Still he said nothing more, so she closed her eyes and let her thoughts encompass sweet memories again.

Then his head lifted and she knew he was looking down at her. "Joanna, I have to know. I want you to . . . I want you to recite the preamble to the Constitution. Can you do that?"

"Is this a pop quiz?" she teased in the darkness.

"No. Just tell me."

"I never learned it," she said dreamily and snuggled deeper into him.

"All right. How about . . . the Declaration of Independence?"

She frowned a little smile, deciding to humor him. Joanna drew a deep breath. "Four score and seven years ago . . . our fathers brought forth on this continent . . . a new nation conceived"—when she reached to stroke his stomach, the muscles rippled beneath her palm—"in liberty . . . and dedicated to the proposition—" Her hand slid down to tease him further.

"God, that's enough." He caught her hand in his.

"Great pillow talk, Simon," she said drowsily, closing her eyes only to have them opened again.

"You won't do that, will you?"

"Won't do what?"

"Conceive."

Her lips barely moved as she told him, "No, I won't do that. Can I go to sleep now?"

She felt a pent-up breath escape him. "Yeah," he whispered, then leaned down to tenderly kiss her nose. "We can both go to sleep now."

As the red morning sun peaked over the horizon, Simon's eyes blinked to the awareness that he was not alone in his bed. He didn't need to turn over and look. He knew who it was. Joanna. Her back was just inches from his. The enticing scent of her hair still lingered seductively in the crisp white of his pillow. He drew a slow, deep breath in appreciation. And though he could've basked for hours in the memory of the night he'd spent with her, Simon got a grip on his emotions, forcing his thoughts to a stern appraisal of this thoroughly unnerving development.

Careful of his movement so as not to wake her, he brought a slow and cautious palm up to push the tousled hair from his forehead before letting it rest at his side. He needed some time to think. My God, what had he done? He'd become involved. That's what he'd done. With a teacher. A colleague. One who lived in his house. Too damned close. He hadn't wanted to become involved. He didn't need that kind of complication in his life. Yet here he was with this woman—a very desirable woman—lying next to him. How awkward! What did it all mean?

Simon closed his eyes. The worst part was that he wanted badly to roll over and kiss her awake, to do it all again. The dumbest move he could ever make, he reasoned, mentally shaking his head. God, she had surprised him. Stunned him, really. He had never expected Joanna—the most confident, if not the cockiest, woman he'd ever known—to be so vulnerable, so soft and giving in his arms. He felt strangely obligated to her now. He didn't know how exactly, he just did. Hell, he wasn't good at this sort of thing. His fists clenched at his new sense of protectiveness, responsibility, toward her, both emotions he hadn't wanted to feel. He sighed. . . .

Gradually aware of the strange firmness of the mattress beneath her, Joanna squinted, noting the unfamiliarity of the bureau, the cushioned valet, the entire room, then closed her eyes again, realizing where she was and how she had come to be there. As she listened to his even breathing, her memory stirred with affection as it all came back. The wonderful night she had spent with Simon. The things he had done with his mouth, his tongue, his hands. The way he had responded with such earthy intensity, such exciting passion. It was sheer ecstasy.

But a questioning frown slowly overtook the curve of her lips as she remembered with disturbing clarity the way *she* had responded. She had never felt more possessed, more vulnerable than she had in Simon's arms. It was a new experience, almost frightening that he could make her enjoy him with such abandon. She wasn't a child. She was a woman. But he had made her feel more like a woman than she'd ever felt before. What was worse, she felt very much like *his* woman.

Would he see it that way, she wondered. Would he

now expect her to be his, any time he wanted her? She wasn't sure she wanted that. How awkward to be living in the same house. It might be confining. And yet she toyed seriously with the idea of waking Simon to relive it all again. But only for a moment. Much as she wanted that, Joanna knew it would be the wrong thing to do just now.

Turning slowly onto her back, she stared at the ceiling, loving his fierceness, his intensity. At the same time, she feared those qualities, or rather feared her own reaction to them. Still, perhaps things could work out, she reasoned. It would be best to get out of his bedroom and wait to see which way the wind blew. She would put on her robe and—damn! Joanna sighed, wishing she'd had the foresight to bring it. Now she really was vulnerable.

She felt him shifting to face her. As she turned her cheek to the pillow, she managed a hesitant smile. "Hello there."

His green eyes seemed brighter, more probing in the morning light, his sleep-tossed hair oddly endearing. As though he sensed her thoughts, Simon combed long fingers through the toasty richness. The look was still endearing, she decided stubbornly. She wanted badly to reach out and stroke the manly jaw, roughened by a night's growth of beard. But she didn't. His expression was decidedly grim. Instinctively, Joanna clutched the sheet that covered her breasts, but left his muscular chest exposed.

"Good morning." His voice was husky with sleep as he offered a smile of his own—a small one. "I didn't expect you to wake up so early."

"A fluke, I suppose."

She felt the heat of his gaze slide over her from head to toe, searing through the sheet to the bare skin beneath before he looked away. "You look—you look very pretty in the morning." The compliment was almost grudging.

He didn't have to be so depressed about it, she thought wryly. Then there was silence between them. Dropping her own gaze, she lifted a fingertip to stroke the gentle arch of her brow. Simon raised himself to a sitting position, propping a pillow before settling himself against it. She was just about to ask if he wouldn't mind getting her robe when he spoke again.

"Joanna, we need to talk—"

"Could you get me my robe?" Looking past him, Joanna spied his black one, draped across the Windsor chair near the bed.

"In a minute. Let me say this now while it makes some kind of sense. About last night . . ." Clearing his throat, Simon seemed to search for words that would spare her feelings. She appreciated that—a little. But the fact that he thought they *needed* sparing bothered her—a lot. "What we shared last night was nice . . . *very* nice," he said quite soberly, and then frowned thoughtfully as his voice dropped to a whisper. "But I think we both know that it shouldn't have happened. After all, you'll be leaving. Nothing can come of it."

She didn't stop to analyze whether it was real disappointment or merely wounded vanity that caused her stomach to tighten. But Joanna drew herself up to sit too, pulling the sheet with her as she leaned against the headboard. It was true. She would be leaving. And maybe nothing could come of it. He made perfect sense. Perfect *Simon* sense.

"We don't live our lives the same way," he was saying. "Or like the same things. It just wouldn't work. The differences are obvious."

Nodding agreement that she suddenly didn't feel at all, Joanna wondered who needed more convincing. "You're right, Simon. I mean, my God, you take everything so seriously. I suppose I'm rather casual."

Not quite sure what she meant by that, he was nevertheless grateful for any support she gave to his theory. "You're a junk-food junkie—*and* a nibbler," he accused lightly, wondering what the *hell* that had to do with anything. But Simon forged ahead more calmly. "I, on the other hand, like balanced meals. Three times a day."

"Of course, and you—you wash as you go along," she said, thinking she might just as well jump right in there and offer her own lame contrasts. "I can't face the kitchen without a nap first."

"Yes, and you sleep late. I get up early."

She swung him a pointed glance. "You have something to wear and I don't."

"Now, that's just the kind of thing I'm talking about," he said sincerely. "You're impulsive. I plan ahead."

Well aware that her awkward position offered proof of that particular point, Joanna was nevertheless irritated by his calling attention to it. She looked down in an absent study of her nails. "I'm tolerant. You're not. You're rather stuffy. I'm not," she countered, and enjoyed both his sudden intake of breath and the impatient frown that came with it.

"Don't start with me, Joanna. Let's at least be civil."

"Yes, well, no one could ever accuse you of being uncivil, Simon."

"I was talking about you," he said coolly. "This isn't easy for me, you know. I'm not a man who can easily enter into a casual affair with no thought to the future. I'm not made that way." He sighed his great frustration of that admission. "But there's one thing I'd like to know . . . you don't have to answer if you don't want to—"

"No, I wasn't a virgin," she tossed.

The bed bounced as Simon threw back the covers. "Oh, God," he said, swinging his legs to the floor. *"That* wasn't what I was going to ask."

Joanna shrugged. "Sorry. What was it?"

"Never mind." Wrapping his robe around him and pulling the sash tight, Simon turned back to her. "I would *never* have asked something like that. God, I wish you hadn't told me that."

"Live with it, Simon. Right now I'm in no mood for modesty."

He didn't want to know such personal things about her. It made him feel even more protective. It brought a closeness that he didn't want. The jeer at himself was swift and sure. You idiot. You made love to her. He stole another glance at the woman in his bed, the sheet outlining her feminine curves. How much closer could a man and woman get? Lots, he admitted grimly. Lots.

"Look, this is really getting us nowhere," he said, pushing his hands into the pockets of his bathrobe.

"I know that, Simon," she agreed wholeheartedly. "So why don't we just call ourselves friends and leave it at that?"

"Friends?" Doubt laced his tone as he returned to sit

on the edge of the bed. "I don't believe any man and woman can be busom buddies. I've never been able to do that with a woman. There are inherent differences between men and women that make real friendship untenable. No." He shook his head. "I'm not at all sure it's possible."

She stared at his broad back for a long moment, wondering how such a man could have made it this far into the twentieth century. Friendships with men? She'd rarely had anything else with them. To hell with her robe. Joanna swept the covers aside and got up to walk around the bed toward the door. "Oh, it's possible, Simon. Take my word for it."

As she made her way back to her side of the house, Joanna knew it was entirely possible. She'd been a pal more times than she cared to remember. First in the hearts of men who needed to discuss *women* troubles. Most of her relationships with men *had* been casual. Could she help it if she had hoped for something more with Simon? It didn't have to be permanent. She wasn't asking for that. Her traveling, her work, kept her too busy for something like . . . marriage. She wanted to be warmed by the fires of passion, but not consumed by them.

Joanna washed and dressed in jeans and a pullover shirt, her thoughts remaining unmercifully on Simon. She'd be damned if she would chase this man—although she'd never met a man who was more in need of chasing. She doubted he could be caught any other way. But *she* wouldn't be the one to do it. No, she wouldn't be the one.

As she guided the comb through her dark hair, though, Joanna wanted badly to show him that her way of living wasn't so awful. She wanted to show him that things didn't have to be thought out to death. Life didn't have to be lived according to one long master plan, without deviation.

Replacing the comb on the dresser, Joanna stared hard into the mirror. Yes, she thought, he needed to be shown that his way wasn't the only way. As she considered the possibilities, confidence slowly curved her lips into a wistful smile. Now she might consider being the one to do *that*. Maybe.

CHAPTER SIX

From a chair at the back of the room, he watched her. Each time his thoughts strayed, Simon forced his eyes to a businesslike gaze again. He'd come to observe—or so he'd told her. Joanna's lecture to a consumer economics class had hardly begun, but he was already impressed.

Her petiteness was more pronounced by the lectern she stood behind. As though sensing that, she gradually moved to perch on the edge of a long, low table. Simon looked away from that most intriguing point where her hips made contact with the wood. Slowly he let his gaze wander back to her, though, knowing he couldn't stare at the wall indefinitely, for God's sake.

Joanna's presence lured, rather than commanded. Some twenty students—most of them male—offered rapt attention, he noticed. It might've been the melodic huskiness in her voice that held them captive. Or maybe the occasional anecdotes she injected into an otherwise somber subject. She was obviously knowledgeable. Thoroughly entertaining. Articulate too. But then he was well acquainted with her ability to drive home a point.

She'd worn a dress today—a gray wool, with wide white lapels. It faithfully followed the curve of her breasts and the trim line of her waist. She looked damn good. So why did he keep thinking back to a time—a more intimate time—when she had worn nothing at all?

Shifting in the chair, he tried not to see dark hair tumbling down a creamy bare back. It was too distracting. Or moist, petulant lips curving slowly to trusting surrender. It was too easy to conjure the feel of gently sloping hips and long, shapely legs wrapped seductively around him. Perversely, he held on as the image and all the pleasure he associated with it moved out of his reach, his vision, much the way it had when she'd walked from his bed that morning, almost three weeks before.

A collective ripple of laughter undulated through the room. He smiled absently, drawn back to the present and to her.

"I think we have a few minutes for discussion," she said, checking the dainty band of silver at her wrist.

Simon hoped no one would want discussion. He was ready to see her alone for a few minutes. But he knew he was about to be frustrated when a young man he recognized from one of his own classes began to speak.

Listening with half an ear, Simon let his thoughts stray again to that morning when they'd agreed to be "just friends." Several times since then, she'd given him cause to rethink the things he'd said—though not to the point of retraction. But the certain conviction he'd felt at the time had weakened over the past few weeks. God, who wouldn't weaken with a woman like her? She was such a creature of impulse. In a split second she decided what she wanted and then blindly went after it.

He remembered the day they stopped at a local mall to take advantage of a sale on light bulbs. His plan was to get the bulbs and go straight home. But outside the hardware store, Joanna had happened to glance up at the marquee of the theater next door and decided right then that she must see the movie playing. She saw no earthly reason to wait, no reason why he shouldn't see it too, even though he had a lecture to prepare, even though she had an article for the local newspaper to finish. All that had meant nothing in the face of a Paul Newman poster. They saw the movie.

"I guess that's all for today," she was saying.

Even after dismissal, some students lingered, gathering at her desk with questions about the assignment, perhaps—he didn't know. But they seemed to like and respect her. He could understand that. He liked her too.

Now that he thought about it, Simon guessed she was rather amusing, if at times exasperating. She had a way of magically making his reasonable rationale look like petty protest, a plot to somehow deny her pleasure.

He didn't know exactly how she did it. But she did. It was the same when they'd shopped for groceries together. Somewhere between the frozen foods and the fresh vegetables she'd coaxed an unwise admission from him. He had conceded that, yes, devil's food cake made a nice dessert. But it was the more nutritional fresh apricots that went into his shopping cart. With one slow shake of her head, Joanna made him feel like a hypocrite. He'd lamely replaced the fruit and followed her back to the bakery section. Despite all that, Simon admired her candor, her knack for turning every excursion into an adventure. She said what she meant and meant what she said—at least for the moment she said it.

Aware of the warm tingle that ambled down his spine, he looked her way again. Alone now, she was staring at him from across the room, a question glinting in the blue of her eyes.

"Did I pass? What did you think?"

As she came toward him, Simon looked down at his notes. There were none. Doodled hearts, elaborate bouquets and the name *Joanna* in bold script stared back at him. My God. He closed his notebook and stood up.

"It went very well," he said tentatively. "Informative, entertaining, comprehensive. Yes, it went very well," he said, more certainly.

"Good. I'm glad you enjoyed it. Now, how about giving me a ride home?" she said. "I walked this morning, you know."

He knew only too well. He'd warned her that it was going to rain, but Joanna had insisted on doing it her way. By coincidence he happened to be dusting the venetian blinds at his window when she'd set out, black clouds hovering over her like Titans waiting to strike. Yet not a drop of water had dampened that confidence she wore like a suit of armor. Oh, it had rained all right. But not until midmorning when she was safely inside her classroom. Simon could hardly believe the incredible luck she enjoyed.

They stopped off at their respective offices to collect their things before meeting again in the corridor. The sky was still overcast as he walked beside her out to the faculty parking lot. Passing other college personnel leaving for the day, Simon couldn't help wondering if any of them suspected his relationship with Joanna— although there *was* no relationship, he reminded himself. Still he wondered if it showed, what he had done with her, what—at times—he ached to do again.

Instinctively, he moved closer to her and then, thinking better of the protective action, forced himself to maintain a more casual distance. It would be best to keep his mind on the test papers he'd planned to grade that evening, he thought grimly.

Simon unlocked the car door for her and then moved to the back of the station wagon to open the tailgate. Placing his umbrella inside, he noticed the water dripping from the brown headliner fabric that covered the inside roof onto some folders he'd left in the car.

"Damn," he muttered, shifting the stack to a dry spot before going around to seat himself behind the wheel.

"What is it?" she asked as he turned the key.

"Another leak," he murmured impatiently. "Or rather the same leak. It's been there ever since I bought the car."

"So why don't you have it fixed?"

"I have. Three times. Each time they tell me it's been repaired, I believe them—until it rains again, of course." He lifted one shoulder in a shrug. "Guess I'll have to make an appointment with the dealer and try again."

"An appointment?" She rolled her eyes. "They hardly deserve that courtesy. Why don't we go over there now? Doesn't that make you angry?"

"Yes, but I—"

111

"Well, then, let's go. I'm not busy. You shouldn't let them take advantage of you like that."

"No one's taking advantage," he defended. "I'll take care of it."

She was silent for a long and meaningful moment. Simon detected a certain feminine scorn in the way she crossed her arms over her shapely breasts.

"I take it you disapprove," he said, and then wished he hadn't given her such an easy opening.

She stared ahead. "All I know is that you obviously didn't listen very closely to my lecture on prompt consumer action when products *and* services are faulty."

She was right about that, he admitted—silently. But if he *had* listened, he most probably would've disagreed, he decided. "What would you have me do, Joanna? Drive to the dealership and punch out the service manager?"

She offered a glance meant to wither. "That's hardly necessary," she said. He thought her tone rather pompous. "If one knows how it's done, one can get satisfactory results."

"And I suppose you think you know how it's done," he mused.

"You bet I do."

She seemed so eager to prove it that Simon turned the car around at the first opportunity and drove straight to the dealer. She deserved this, he thought, dutifully answering her questions about the leak, providing details of previous visits to the small dealership and the subsequent excuses for each failure.

Joanna was unimpressed, he noticed. Still Simon felt almost guilty about throwing her into the ring with Lewis Granger, the burly service manager and longtime

112

acquaintance of Simon's. Lewis was normally a good-natured man, but he didn't like to be told his business—especially by a woman. He would have no qualms at all about putting an irate, uninformed and therefore "uppity" female in her proper place.

By the time he pulled the car up to the wide overhead door of the service area, Simon had changed his mind and started to warn her. But when she reached across and laid on the horn, releasing a loud, long blast, he decided she needed the lesson in tolerance that she was most assuredly about to get.

The big door drew slowly upward to reveal Lewis—feet set in a wide stance, bushy brows knitted in stern reprimand. When big hands crisscrossed an overblown chest to tuck themselves beneath Lewis's armpits, Simon wondered if Lewis ever had the urge to carry a cutlass.

Joanna got out of the car before he could stop her, approaching Lewis with a confidence never before seen in man or beast, Simon decided ruefully. He thought about staying there behind the wheel to let her take the medicine. But again he was seized by the damnable protective instinct and so joined the two of them at the entrance to the shop.

"Lew, I'm afraid we've got a real problem here," she was saying.

Simon glanced a knowing apology to the man she was saying it to. Nobody called Lewis Granger Lew. Usually he made it plain that he didn't like his name shortened. But Lewis didn't acknowledge Simon's look. The service manager was too busy giving Joanna a thoroughly skeptical once-over.

"After three visits to this dealership, the roof of Dr.

Gregory's new station wagon still leaks," she went on. "Now I'm sure you'll agree that he's been patient. But this can't be allowed to continue. It's clear that either you don't have the right equipment or you don't possess the know-how to find the cause of the problem." She stopped, obviously waiting for Lewis to address the charge.

After a long pause, Lewis let go of the stern fix he had on Joanna and turned an inquiring frown to Simon. "Who is this person?" he asked. But before Simon could answer, Joanna held out a hand.

"Sorry, Lew. I didn't introduce myself. Joanna Sinclair's the name."

Lewis kept both hands on his hips, eying her with patent disdain.

Ignoring his refusal to shake her hand, Joanna quickly brought it back to her side. "Now, as I see it, there are several approaches one might take in solving the problem. Come on back here, Lew." Turning away, Joanna crooked a finger and Simon wondered if Lewis might not reach up and break it off. "I assume you've already tried resealing the rear window," she said.

Lewis answered with a grudging grunt, but he followed her to the back of the car, apparently curious about her sensible assumption.

"But what about the headliner? Have you removed that for inspection?" she asked.

"We do that only as a last resort," the service manager grumbled, displaying more patience than Simon had ever witnessed.

"Wouldn't you say we're down to that?" she asked, her blunt question clearing Simon's throat with caution. "To be honest, Lew, I think it's time you brought in a factory rep on this one." Despite the sudden stiffening in the big man's shoulders, Joanna opened the tailgate, reaching inside to the headliner. "This fabric is soaked," she pointed out. "There could be some bad spot welds where the luggage carrier was attached." Rubbing the dampness from her palms, Joanna nudged the door closed and faced him again. "Now, what do you say, Lew?"

Again Lewis stared hard, his jaw working as though he was imagining the great satisfaction of chewing her up and spitting her out. But slowly, to Simon's surprise, a slight grudging smile formed as Lewis's chin zig-zagged downward in wonder. "How do you know so much?"

She returned a modest smile of her own, one shoulder lifting in a charming shrug. "It's part of my business to know, Mr. Granger. I've done some studies on the auto-mobile industry and the problem of leaky station wag-ons isn't uncommon. I'm sure you realize that. We'll take a loaner until it's repaired," she finished.

A short lift of bushy brows was his only concession as the service manager walked back to where Simon stood. "The factory rep will be here from St. Louis day after tomorrow," he muttered. "Meanwhile, we'll take a look at the welding."

A wait of two more days, perhaps more, would mean further inconvenience. Simon decided to deal with that later. Right now he was concerned with other things. Like how in the hell Joanna had commanded this kind of response when all he'd received were excuses. And why the hell Lewis hadn't told her that *he* was the ser-vice manager and as such would decide how to handle the problem.

"Well, *Lew,*" he said with light sarcasm, "I guess I'll have to live with that, won't I?" Simon took Granger's arm and walked him deeper into the garage. "Is anything wrong today, Lewis. You seem . . . subdued."

Lewis tipped his chin in resignation. "It's no use arguing with a woman like that—especially one who's right and knows it."

"Hmm. I guess I expected you to somehow take her down a peg or two." His own best interests to the contrary, Simon realized with great confusion that secretly he'd been rooting for Lewis all along. In any case, he didn't think Joanna ought to be encouraged.

As though sensing that, the other man let out a sly, calculating chuckle. "Well, don't feel too badly, Dr. Gregory. The sad truth is . . . we're all out of loaners."

Despite the fact that he would now have to pay cab fare or walk home, Simon felt oddly pleased by that admission—rather smug, actually. Clapping Lewis Granger's shoulder, Simon said good-bye and went out to inform Joanna that, because of her insistence, her utter lack of planning, she had rendered them both without transportation.

"In other words, we're afoot," he said pointedly.

"It isn't that far. We'll walk," she returned easily. "It's a great day for it."

Simon's eyes narrowed in total exasperation. Dammit, nothing seemed to rattle her. Nothing. And it was a lousy day for walking. Watching her look up at him, point-blank assurance lending unadulterated sparkle to the blue of her eyes, Simon didn't know whether to kiss her or pinch her.

Deciding that either could lead to something he

wasn't prepared to deal with right now, he merely let out a deep breath and took his umbrella from the car. She assured him he wouldn't need it. He took it anyway and set off beside her toward home. Simon was almost glad when, before they had walked a block, huge drops of chilling rain began to pelt them. It gave him good reason to glare at her the rest of the way.

Stretching his arms over his shoulders, Simon vented a yawn at the typewriter, then relaxed again. He didn't really want to prepare a lecture today. But he would. Because he was a responsible person. Not like some other people he could name. No matter that the first sunshine in days was spilling through his bedroom window, he reasoned. No matter that Joanna was outside taking advantage of a fairly warm Sunday afternoon.

Still, he spared a look past the breeze-blown curtains to the patio where she stood, hands on shapely hips, surveying the cloudless sky. He was almost certain she had work to do too. And he wished she would go back inside and do whatever it was she found so easy to disregard.

When she wandered off toward the garage, he lifted his fingers back to the typewriter keys and forced his focus on the matter at hand. Before long his typing had developed a smooth rhythm, his thoughts a natural sequence. Yes, sir, he was clipping right along, he thought smugly. Then an irritating scratch on the window screen interrupted everything. With a sigh, he lifted the paper bail to read over what he had written.

"Hey, you in there."

"What is it, Joanna?"

"I found a basketball. All I need is an air pump and I'm in business."

"Hanging from a nail on the wall by the lawn mower," he said.

"Thanks." Then she was gone again.

But soon the rhythmic twang of an overinflated basketball slapping against the driveway shattered his concentration. Simon rose and wandered toward the window to watch Joanna. Dressed in a hooded sweat shirt and jeans, she worked her way down an imaginary court to lob the ball toward the hoop above the garage door.

She could dribble all right, he conceded, but she couldn't shoot worth a damn. Again and again she tried, but the ball either ricocheted off the rim of the hoop or missed it completely, bouncing on the garage roof only to roll back into her arms—she was fairly good at catching it. After a few moments, Simon pulled himself back to his desk. But when he finally heard the swish of the net for two points, he silently cheered her.

Before he'd composed another paragraph, the grating scratch sounded again. "Want to play horse?" she asked.

"No, thanks," he muttered, making the correction on the page, irritated with the need for it. "That's for amateurs."

"Whoa," she teased. "I didn't know I was dealing with a pro. How about a little one-on-one, Wilt?"

A breath of exasperation preceded his turn to the window once more. Curved palms wreathed her eyes, just visible above the bottom of the sash as she peered inside to warn him. Simon smiled, in spite of himself. "You know, you're awfully cocky for someone who makes one shot in ten. But maybe I will come out and show you how to handle the ball. Be there in a minute."

"Great." Dribbling back to the driveway, Joanna was thrilled that he had decided to join her. He could handle the ball all he wanted. She would handle *him*. While waiting for Simon, she took several practice shots, missing all but two. Then he appeared, looking awfully competitive in his sweat shirt, jeans and tennis shoes.

"All right, Dr. J.," he said, surrounding her with an aggressive guarding stance, "show me your stuff."

She presented her most awesome stare.

He was unimpressed.

She growled.

He laughed.

Although she was no match for him, Joanna didn't allow herself to be intimidated by his size or the maddening way he blocked every shot she tried. This was the closest he'd been to her in days and she intended to enjoy him and his appealing masculine scent to the fullest. With no effort at all, he made goal after goal. But she didn't care.

When it was her turn to shoot, Joanna frequently turned away from Simon and then backed up, dribbling right into his thighs. His cries of foul were insignificant compared to the pleasing sensation of having his arms around her, his breath tingling her neck, each time he struggled to regain his balance. Still, there seemed no way to get past his long arms. He bounced the ball right out of her grasp several times. Finally, it was her turn again.

In desperation, Joanna halted suddenly, her eyes widening as she turned toward the patio and gasped, "Oh, my God, I think someone's in the kitchen."

When Simon automatically pivoted in that direction, she dribbled smugly past him and lobbed the ball for her one and only basket of the game. "Time out," she called conveniently.

With clumsy attempts to spin the basketball on her fingertip, she passed regally beneath his dry stare on her way to the patio. Once there she sank wearily onto the chaise longue and lifted her hair off her neck to allow the cool air access.

"Now that's what I call rousing," she said, her attention now on regaining control of her breathing.

"Funny," he said, following with wry amusement. "That's what I call cheating."

She dipped her chin in a tease. "What's a little one-on-one without subterfuge?"

Simon went into the kitchen and returned with remnants of a smile and two glasses of ice water. Joanna didn't particularly want the one he held out to her, but she took it, simply because he'd made the gesture.

"Thank you," she said, drawing her knees up to make room for him at the end of the chaise. When he sat, the material of his jeans stretched tight across muscular thighs that had expanded with exercise. Her eyes were drawn as always to the toasty hair that now lay in roguishly tossed layers, the attractive jaw that appeared even stronger with the faint sheen of perspiration. Joanna looked away. "You're pretty good at basketball," she said. "Did you play in school?"

"Not on a team," he admitted with a reminiscent shrug. "I *wanted* to." Then Simon turned to her, a totally false stoicism in the set of his mouth. "I never could master the lay-up, Joanna."

"Ah." She nodded, frowning her thoughtful amusement. "I know what you mean. I guess we all have our own cross to bear," she said with an exaggerated sigh. "I wanted to be a cheerleader. But somehow I never could do the splits."

"Never?" he teased.

"Umm, I think I did once, but it might've been all in my imagination—I fantasized a lot back then. Still do, on occasion." This time her sigh held no pretense at all.

Masculine fingers reached slowly to her ankle to hold, then gently caress the sensitive skin there. "About what, Joanna?"

The deep whisper of his voice drew her gaze to his eyes. For a moment she was caught in an emerald question, lured by uncertain regard. But she wasn't about to confess that it was he who completely filled her fantasies these days, although it would have been the greatest truth she'd ever spoken. Despite his question, Simon wasn't ready to hear the answer. She didn't know if he would ever be ready. He didn't seem to have room for a woman in his life right now.

And so Joanna smiled, biting her lip to stop its slightest quiver. "Lots of things, Simon," she said quietly. "Lots of things."

Sensing that he might have done something not quite fair, Simon slid his hand from her warm skin and brought it back to rest on his knee. He was glad she had dragged him outside. Joanna seemed to know intuitively when he needed company. Even when he didn't know himself. Or perhaps she had the uncanny ability to *convince* him he needed her. Either way, he'd enjoyed the past half hour.

"Thanks for the game, Joanna. I feel more relaxed now."

"Good. Perhaps you should get back to your lecture then. Meanwhile, I think I'll make myself a mile-high chocolate sundae."

"You'll spoil your dinner," he warned.

She shrugged her complete indifference. "It won't be the end of the world. In fact, I may bring my ice cream out here and fritter the rest of this wonderful day away."

"Don't you have things to do?" he asked casually, but Joanna was well aware of the hint of disapproval in his voice.

"Um-hmm. Some reading and an article to finish. But there's no hurry. I'll get to it this evening after my nap."

"Oh." Nodding slowly, Simon kept the frown from his face until he was in his room again. He liked Joanna. He *wanted* Joanna. Very much. But, God, he'd never known a woman who lived more haphazardly. Hers was a strictly hit-or-miss existence. And that was all right sometimes. But at other times, he couldn't help wishing they had more in common. That she had more direction. That she was more like him. But she cared nothing for the everyday things that made his own life run smoothly: order, responsibility, self-discipline. She laughed in the face of silly things like health and nutrition. Simon smiled, shaking his head in wonder at her eating habits.

Still, an idea began to form as he returned to his place at the typewriter. Maybe there was something he could do to get her back on the straight and narrow. A symposium on time management was scheduled for the next weekend at Houghton. He could start with that. As a surprise. Who could tell? She might thank him. Simon rolled his eyes at the unlikelihood of that. But he was going to get her there anyway. After all, that's what friends were for.

"I shaved my legs for this, Simon."

Joanna turned her droll expression straight ahead and tried to subdue her growing irritation with the man sitting beside her. So this was his big surprise. A lecture on managing her time. Who did he think he was? The Great Reformer?

Simon's mouth came very close to her ear. "You have to admit that I did tell you the theme of this symposium," he whispered.

"Don't you think *From Here to Eternity* is a little misleading?" she demanded, and then bore the brunt of several shushes from those around her.

The hall was only half filled. Apparently, lots of people had found plenty to do with their time that evening. The second speaker droned on, but Joanna wasn't listening. She was leaving. Pushing herself up from her chair, she nudged past Simon's knees and into the aisle. She knew he was following her to the back of the auditorium. When he caught up with her and took hold of her arm, she kept walking.

"Joanna, this is silly." Still, he pushed open the door and let her pass to the outside.

"Is it?" she asked, moving on to the parking lot and her El Camino. "I know what you're trying to do, Simon. And frankly, I resent it."

He said nothing on the way home. With only fleeting glimpses of an unrepentant profile, Joanna was unable to assess his mood, but guessed he was quite irritated that his plan hadn't worked out. She drove in the darkness, reviewing the past several days. She'd suspected he was trying to change her. All the subtle signs were there. The loan of his vacuum cleaner when she hadn't even asked. Invitations to full-course meals in his dining room. Copies of his favorite book on self-discipline placed at strategic points throughout the house.

She had wanted to think he was just being nice. But now, three well-balanced meals and half a symposium later, she realized the extent of his determination to fit her into some kind of mold. His mold. Well, she liked herself the way she was, thank you. Aware of the knot of disappointment in her chest, she only wished that he liked her that way too.

When she parked the truck in the driveway, Simon caught her wrist and refused to let go. "What's wrong with trying to improve a few personal habits?" he challenged.

"I don't want to discuss my habits, personal or otherwise." Her pulse had begun to pound and she struggled to control it.

"There's nothing wrong with change, Joanna. In fact, there's a lot to be said for reform."

She nodded vigorously. "A lot *has* been said. But I believe Emerson put it best when he wrote, *Every reform was once a private opinion, and when it shall be private again, it will solve the problem of the age.*"

"Aw, Christ." He let go of her wrist and faced forward. "I was only trying to help," he defended. "I thought we were supposed to be friends."

Her tone was cool as she shook her head. "You know, you were born too late, Simon. They could've used you at the Crusades."

"There's no need to get nasty just because you don't understand my motives."

"I think I understand perfectly. You can't change me, Simon. I don't want to change. I'm happy with myself the way I am. That is what *you* don't understand. And I really don't want to hear any more."

Clutching her purse, Joanna got out of the truck and slammed the door, walking purposefully ahead of him into the kitchen.

"There's a casserole on the stove, if you're hungry," he said evenly. Tugging on the knot of his tie, Simon disappeared into his domain, leaving her alone in the room.

Stepping out of her shoes, Joanna wished she hadn't worn them. Or the slinky dress she had chosen. She wished she hadn't put up her hair either. A romantic evening with Simon? Ha! It would never happen. She sighed, lifting the lid on the casserole to stare into a dish of cubed pork and spinach. She replaced the lid, her lip curling instinctively. She was hungry, but she damned sure wasn't going to eat that.

Joanna began to rummage through her stock of canned goods for something more to her liking. She hadn't shopped lately, though. Nothing much on the shelf appealed to her. She decided to try the can of sardines she'd bought on a whim weeks ago.

Simon returned to the kitchen a few minutes later to find her munching a sandwich. He looked around the room as though trying to locate the source of a bad odor.

"Relax, Thumper, the forest is safe," she said dryly.

He leveled a stare at her and then drew a deep breath. "What's that you're eating?"

"A sardine sandwich."

She didn't miss the slightest wince of his eyes as he

125

took the chair opposite her. "Didn't you see my pork and spinach casserole?"

"Yes."

"Well, didn't it look good?"

"It looked like a waste of a perfectly good piece of meat to me."

His chin came up. His shoulders stiffened. "You know, you don't always have to say what's on your mind," he said coolly. "You could show the slightest restraint sometimes. But I take it you don't like spinach."

"You take it right."

"I see. You'd rather eat tiny fish with their heads still on them, huh? And look at the *way* you eat. God, I've never seen such gusto."

She put down her sandwich. "What's wrong with the way I eat? My mother taught me how."

"Mmm-hmm. Your *mother* was married. *You* are single. Single women dine. Married women eat."

"That's a chauvinistic remark if I ever heard one."

"It is not. Since you're so fond of quotes, Erma Bombeck—who, by the wildest stretch of the imagination, could never be called chauvinistic—wrote that in one of her books. I forget which one."

"I read that book too," Joanna countered with an angry nod. "She was quoting her husband! So, *Doctor*, now that you've insulted me, made me madder than hell and ruined my entire evening, you can just go on about your business and leave me in peace!"

"Why is your head bobbing from side to side like that?"

"My head is *not* bobbing," she warned hotly. "That implies that I have no control over it. I assure you I am

126

pushing my head from side to side to emphasize my disgust with you."

"Oh. My mistake. Go ahead and eat your sandwich."

Joanna pushed her chair back to dump the remains of her dinner into the garbage. "I'm—not—hungry." Eyes focused straight ahead, she thrust open the swinging door to waltz through. She felt sick at what he had said. God, she hadn't looked at them carefully. She didn't know the heads were still on the sardines.

CHAPTER SEVEN

For the next few weeks, Simon kept an emotional distance, giving up—outwardly, at least—his mission to change her to his liking. Although they never spoke of the subject, Joanna sensed that, in his way, he was trying to make it up to her. He asked her to go with him to a party at the Hamptons'. A few days later, he invited her to browse at a flea market in Springfield. And when a mid-November storm left a blanket of snow on the community, he wondered aloud if she might like to "bundle up and take a walk." With him.

Not one to hold a grudge, Joanna accepted what she saw as small tokens of his apology. But she wouldn't allow herself to think it was any more than that. He was attentive, charming and, at times, courteous to the point of distraction. Did it mean that he cared? Or did it mean that he couldn't care less? She'd seen him play the polite gentleman with other women, mere acquaintances, who were likely to remain just that in Simon's eyes. She wanted more from him. So much more.

It was this desire that filled her thoughts the day before Thanksgiving, when she should've been packing for the holiday trip to her mother's place in Muskogee. Oklahoma seemed far away now, farther than she wanted to drive that afternoon. The plans were set and yet her mood and her feet dragged.

Lowering the thermostat, she returned to the overstuffed chair by the stereo and opened her book again. But it lay unread on her lap. A fingertip edged along her lower lip and she found herself frowning. On the surface things with Simon were better, and yet, sometimes when he looked at her, a certain expression darkened his eyes. A hint of yearning, perhaps. Disappointment. Tension. She felt it.

Joanna sighed. It was more probably her imagination working overtime, as it had been known to do.

"Joanna?"

She heard Simon's call from the kitchen and knew his entrance would follow immediately. The door swung open. "Joanna? Where are you? I'm ready to leave now."

He was wearing a cable-knit sweater today. A nice brown that highlighted his hair. A down-filled jacket wedged between his arm and ribs, he kept his hands in khaki pockets. When he spotted her and came deeper into the room, his chin tipped slightly as green eyes narrowed in measured surveillance. "I'll be leaving for Topeka in a few minutes. How about you? Did you call your mother?"

"Yes. She's expecting me this evening."

"Will Richard be there for the holidays?"

"Umm." She nodded absently.

One dark brow lifted. He draped his jacket on the back of the sofa and sat on the end nearest her. "Joanna, are you all right? You look a little pale."

"I'm fine," she said, lifting her chin in mild assurance. "It's a little warm in here, but I've adjusted the heat." She smiled at the pleasant, distant sound of her voice. "I'll be leaving soon too." They were going in different directions. Same as always, she thought, a little sad at the prospect of being so far away from him, if only for the next few days.

His gaze casually swept the room before he focused on her again. "Packed yet?"

"I just have to throw a few things in a suitcase and I'll be ready," she said. "Can't wait to get there."

"Oh." He nodded slowly. Simon seemed reluctant to leave. She wished suddenly that he wouldn't.

Stop it, old girl, she told herself. He'd made the plans to visit his parents a month before. "Hadn't you better get going? It's almost a six-hour drive."

"Yes, I suppose I should." Simon stood and claimed his jacket. "Guess I'll see you Sunday." Still, he didn't go. "How long will it take you to get to Muskogee?"

"Not long. Four, maybe four and a half hours." She was becoming a little uncomfortable beneath his visual probe. "See you Sunday, Simon. Have a safe trip."

He drew a deep breath and let it out again. "You, too, Joanna." Finally, he turned and walked from the room.

A few minutes later, faint sounds of a car motor broke the silence and gradually faded away, leaving her alone. Joanna didn't know quite how to feel about that. She was alternately content and then lonely, both emotions tugging within her for control. One thing was certain though. The room had become cold. She was tired. Maybe she should rest some before starting the drive. Maybe she shouldn't go at all. The holiday spirit had completely passed her by.

Suddenly exhausted, Joanna went to the phone and called her mother to give her excuses. "I'm sure it's just a cold," she said when her mother expressed concern that she didn't sound well and disappointment that she would miss the traditional turkey dinner. "I'll be fine," Joanna continued, although her neck had begun to ache with the mere effort of supporting her head. "I just need some rest, that's all. And as for dinner, I'll be home for good next month. You know I wouldn't miss Christmas with you and Richard. Give him my love and I'll see you soon. Good-bye, Mother."

Joanna put down the phone and moved to the sofa to snuggle beneath a warm afghan. Next month. Yes, next month this would all be a memory, she thought drowsily, a shiver tingling her spine. Next month, when she felt better, she would go home. Joanna put up no fight at all when her heavy eyelids closed and she fell into a welcome slumber.

The ringing invaded her dream almost immediately. She tried to push it from her, but it only became louder, more persistent. Opening her eyes to complete darkness, she realized the phone was ringing. When she pushed the hair from her eyes, it was damp and cool in her fingers. The afghan had been shoved aside and she was cold again. With groggy awareness, she dragged herself from the sofa and felt her way past the cocktail table to the phone.

"Hello." Joanna switched on a lamp and squinted.

"Joanna?"

"Simon. It's you." She glanced at her watch but couldn't focus on the face. "What time is it?"

"Almost eleven. Joanna, what's happened? I called your mother and she said you didn't come home because you weren't feeling well."

"Umm." She shivered. "It's just a cold. Go back to bed."

"What? I haven't been to bed." The connection had gone bad. His tone was terse amid the static. "Did you have any dinner?"

"No . . . no." The foreign singsong in her own voice made her frown. "I didn't want any turkey."

There was a pause and she wondered if he was still there.

"I'm coming home right now," he said.

"Oh, don't do that. You'll miss turkey." She sighed. "I guess I could get one, though."

"Forget about the damn turkey, Joanna. Go to bed and stay there."

He was angry. She hadn't meant to make him angry.

"Simon, don't be mad," she coaxed.

His breath crackled over the wire. "Joanna, I'm not mad, sweetheart. Just go to bed and I'll be there when you wake up."

"Okay, I will. 'Bye, Simon."

Joanna felt lighter than she could ever remember feeling. She all but floated into the bedroom to cuddle beneath the covers. Had she imagined the endearment? Or had Simon really said such a nice thing to her? Before she could figure it out, she slept again, a vision of Simon in a down-filled jacket filling her dreams.

When her eyes fluttered open in the morning, he was there, standing over her bed. Her head ached. She felt hot all over, but Joanna managed a welcoming, though weak smile.

"Hi there."

"Hi there, yourself." His voice was soft and deep, soothing to her ears. His mouth, curving into a compassionate expression, was a welcome sight to deprived eyes. He sat on the bed, placing a cool palm to her forehead. There was a flicker of a frown before his smile appeared again. "How do you feel?" he asked, combing dark strands of hair away from her face.

"Better and better," she teased hoarsely.

Simon's eyes closed in a moment of forbearance. Then he opened them again and reached for her hand to squeeze a gentle reprimand. "You should've told me you were sick. I would've stayed with you."

That rather surprised her. "You would?"

"Of course. Don't you know that?"

She didn't know it. She'd never been given a clue.

He offered no excuses for his admission. And she asked for none, preferring to interpret his words herself. But Joanna was glad he didn't say that he came back because she was Richard's sister, or because she was his tenant, or because she a pesky nuisance.

"I think I have a touch of the flu," she said.

He nodded. "I think you're right. But we'll get you well, Joanna . . . starting with lots of rest."

She was deeply touched by the tenderness she heard in his voice, the affection she saw in his eyes. "Thank you, Simon. You're very sweet."

Joanna felt better already, knowing he was there. And his prescription of rest coincided with her own plans. In her limited experience with illness, she had developed quite a successful treatment: Sleep it off.

133

Wake only to gorge the stomach with favorite foods. Then sleep some more. Alternate rest with food until well. It had always worked for her and she looked forward to it now.

Just as she was about to drop off in commencement of that philosophy, he spoke again.

"I'll be back in a few minutes with tea and toast for your breakfast—and some aspirin." When she frowned ever so slightly, Simon sensed that she was about to protest the bother of tea and toast. He touched her lips with a soothing fingertip. "No trouble at all," he assured and then left her.

From that moment on he followed explicitly his mother's advice on nursing Joanna back to health. She slept most of the first day. Between naps, he gave her small doses of chicken soup and Jell-O for her weak stomach. Her protest of his spoon-feeding was only minor, a sign of just how ill she really was, he suspected. Simon woke her at four-hour intervals to give her medicine for her fever.

On the second morning, she was slightly grumpy when he went in to change her bedclothes and tidy the room. But after another breakfast of tea and toast, her droll sense of humor returned. "If I die," she said, "please see that I'm buried beneath a mound of krinkle-cut french fries."

By midafternoon Joanna seemed restless. In keeping with his mother's advice to humor the ill—but against his own judgment—he lay on the water bed with Joanna and read from a steamy novel he'd found on her night table. Almost immediately she fell asleep on his shoulder, though, and he was forced to enjoy the good parts alone. When she snuggled very close, he held her to him, conscious of her hands seeking warmth beneath his sweater. *Acutely* aware of her thigh, which had somehow made its way to his groin.

After one kiss, helplessly pressed to her hair, Simon was reminded vividly of his mother's tactful suggestion —given while writing the recipe for chicken soup—that, despite temptation, it would be unseemly to take advantage of an ill and therefore defenseless woman. But his mother had never met Joanna and as such couldn't know that *he* was the one in danger.

Joanna appreciated his patient ministrations. She really did. But by the third day, she thought if he woke her up once more to give her aspirin or change her sheets, she might burst into tears. He had shot her theory of sleep and food to hell. Although she had improved considerably, she wondered if it was because of or in spite of Simon.

Still, she said nothing about her suspicions. How could she? He'd cooked for her—in a manner of speaking—cleaned for her, nursed her back to health and washed her dirty laundry. Never mind that he'd awakened her twice to express his lack of faith in her fabric softener. He'd even given her a small bell to summon him whenever necessary. Never had any man shown her the kindness, the compassion, the affection that Simon had displayed the past few days. He'd kept this side of himself hidden from her until now. Joanna wasn't about to criticize this gentle and thoroughly endearing man she'd come to know.

So when he caught her washing her hair on Sunday morning, she remained bent over the sink, silent and guilty as he raved.

"My *God!* What the *hell* are you *doing?*" he demanded, grabbing a towel to unceremoniously cover her head in terry cloth and pull her up from the sink. "Don't you know you could catch your death this way?"

Joanna didn't dispute the old wives' tale, but stood still and submitted to the brisk rub of her head. Nor did she protest when he set her down on a stool and dried her hair with her blow dryer. From all the tugging and pulling, she suspected he had little experience with the tool. His apologies were gruff but sincere each time he accidentally banged her head with the barrel.

But by nine o'clock that evening, Joanna was desperate. After another dinner of "liquids," her stomach groaned for something more substantial. She was determined to appease it. Buttoning her knee-length nightshirt of ivory silk, she formed a haphazard plan to sneak into the kitchen while Simon was occupied in his part of the house. She had no wish to offend him, but Joanna was ravenous. With any luck at all, he'd never know.

Barefoot, she moved, quietly but purposefully, into the kitchen and eased on the light switch. Searching the bread box for a cupcake, she found nothing but half a loaf of whole-wheat bread. When the wooden lid snapped shut before she could stop it, Joanna winced at the sound it made. Seconds later, the door swung open and she turned, defeated, to face Simon, an open book folded over the arm of his vee-neck sweater.

"Joanna, I thought I heard you in here. Can I get you anything? You should've rung the bell."

He was doing it again. Being so nice that she couldn't hurt his feelings. But she was starving. Absolutely starving. "I don't need the bell anymore, Simon. I think I'm well now. I just came in for a . . . snack."

"Oh." He closed the book and set it on the cabinet. "There's some Jell-O left over from dinner. Would you—"

"No," she said as casually as her stomach would allow. "That isn't what I need."

"Applesauce?" he suggested, as though he were certain that would hit the spot.

She looked away, biting her lip in restraint. But a sigh escaped and she knew it was no use. "Meat, Simon. I need meat. And potatoes. French fries."

"Oh, Joanna, that would turn your stomach inside out."

"No, it wouldn't," she assured with a vigorous shake of her head. "My stomach would be thrilled." Joanna tried to remain calm, but it wasn't easy. "Simon, I appreciate everything you've done but . . . I think my teeth are getting soft. I haven't used them in almost four days. If I don't get a cheeseburger soon, I'll die."

"Joanna . . ." he protested mildly, offering a sideways glance of suspicion.

"I mean it, Simon. I really mean it."

His sigh was almost a groan. "I honestly don't think you're ready for that, but if you insist—I'll go out and get you something. What would you like? Cheeseburger and fries? Pizza? A box of fried chicken?"

She brightened immediately. "Yes."

He frowned his disbelief. "All that?"

"And a chocolate shake." Again she looked away. "Jumbo." Her stomach began to stir in anticipation. "Go to the Burger Palace on Ashland. They—know me there."

The moment he was gone, Joanna began to make the necessary preparations for the impending feast. She went straight to the refrigerator and took out the ketchup. Placing the bottle in the center of the kitchen table, she sat down and tried to get control of her emotions.

Simon found her there a half hour later, her hands folded calmly on the table. On the way to the Burger Palace, he'd come to terms with the fact that despite his hope, she wasn't ever going to like applesauce. Resigned, he aligned three paper bags in a neat row before her.

"Joanna, go easy at first," he said dryly, removing his jacket and hanging it on the back of the chair next to hers before he sat down. "I don't want you to OD on your recovery."

When Joanna tore into the foil-wrapped cheeseburger and took it straight to her mouth, he knew she must be well. Her coordination had returned too, he noticed, watching in wonder. With no trouble at all, Joanna chewed, swallowed and helped herself to great sips of a shake, all the while ripping into the box of chicken. Wolfing down the food, she halfheartedly held out her fries to him.

He smiled. "I'll pass."

God, she loved him for that. "You're wonderful," she said, popping another krinkle-cut into her mouth. Simon was staring as though mesmerized, but she couldn't concern herself with that now. She'd been too long without sustenance. He seemed to understand. The pizza was smothered in pepperoni. Although she ate only one piece, her thoughts raced with plans for a midnight rendezvous.

When the meal was over, she sat back and took a deep breath of supreme satisfaction. She could live now.

"Thanks, Simon," she said, letting her sincere gratitude come forth. "Thanks for being so nice to me. I'll clear the table in just a minute."

"I don't know," he said, his eyes alert with amusement. "Maybe we should leave this mess. As a sort of memorial to what went on here tonight."

She smiled rather shyly, delighted by his teasing. The smile led the way to a chuckle filled with affection for him.

"Come into the living room while I get the fire going again," he invited, taking her hand to pull her up from the chair.

She followed him gladly and stood at the hearth as he added another log to the fireplace. He reached for the poker, blue denim stretching attractively across his thighs as he knelt to stoke the flames. As she watched the fire's reflection play over his hair in shimmering highlights, Joanna wasn't surprised at the steady rise in her pulse rate. To her it had become a natural reaction whenever he was near. Now that one appetite had been sated, her thoughts, her wishes turned to another. The one that had gone unrequited for months. He cared for her. She knew he did. And she cared very much for him.

Replacing the poker in its metal stand, Simon stood, one hand in his pocket as he stared pensively into the blaze. After a moment he smiled. "I admire you, Joanna," he whispered. "Sometimes I wish I could be more like you. You and your impulse. You and your spontaneous combustion."

The admission threw her, but she rallied, turning her own focus to the fire. "I'd be interested to know what

139

impulse you're fighting right now." Joanna felt his gaze and met the uncertainty in his eyes.

"The one that's telling me to kiss you, hold you . . . make love to you."

"Umm." Her winsome smile was soft and searching. "That's a battle I hope you lose," she said quietly, a bit breathless at the prospect. "Would it help if I told you that I very much *want* you to do all those things?"

He shook his head slowly. "I think I just lost." His hands came up to tenderly cup her face.

"We'll both win, Simon. We can't help but win."

Just before his lips met hers, Joanna drew a broken breath of hope into her lungs. His mouth was sweet and warm on hers, expressing the need she herself had kept under control for so long. She felt lost when he stayed only for a moment.

He'd gone to the sofa to begin removing several throw pillows, dropping each one to the rug in front of the hearth. Then he came back to her, his eyes, his mouth, his hands encouraging. With trembling fingers, she eased his sweater up past his shoulders and over his head, smoothing his hair with one hand as the other dropped the argyle wool to the rug. Simon removed his shoes and the rest of his clothes.

And when he stood naked and beautiful before her, she saw for the first time things her hands had already experienced in darkness. The fine symmetry of Simon. The sloping muscles of his chest and the soft mat of curling hair there. The firm, flat stomach and the manly, seductive fire below. The thirst of her eyes unquenchable, she drank the masculine contours, the trim hips and athletic thighs above thoroughly intriguing calves.

140

As he moved slowly toward her, Joanna again focused on his eyes and the great desire offered up from emerald depths. Her breathing increased measurably. The mere touch of his hands on her arms drew her to him. He kissed her again and she knew this was going to be different from anything she'd ever experienced.

He took his time removing her nightshirt, working the buttons, one by one, to kiss each strip of the flesh revealed to him. His mouth moved down to the sensitive skin of her stomach, his tongue drawing to the surface desire that had smoldered for months. She felt the silk slide from her shoulders, past her waist and hips to surround her feet at the floor. As Joanna stepped out of her gown, her breasts were warmed exquisitely by the touch of his hand on them.

A possessive palm caressed her nape as he drew her down among the cushions where he lay facing her. The firelight cast dancing shadows along his thighs as she reached for that part of him to run tender fingers along the muscled flesh. The fine hair tickled.

He reached for a nubbed pillow and placed it gently beneath her head. Leaning over her, Simon put a searing fingertip to the underside of one breast and drew fire in his slow path around it. She glanced at his mouth and saw its yearning.

Joanna received his kiss with an eager restraint, wanting, needing to take time to enjoy this new way of loving Simon. She had known once his earthy passion. His unleashed intensity. Now she discovered that he could be slow, coaxing and exquisitely tender. And so she was with him.

In the long, delirious encounters that followed, they exchanged uninhibited, poignant knowledge of each

141

other. His tongue serenaded her mouth with a sweet song of love, a duet of their bodies, their souls, entwining to make the music. His flirting feet courted her toes to a reflexive curling. His chest pressed into her breasts as she welcomed the pleasant weight of him, the cozy, impassioned warmth of him. The special intimacy, the enchanting communication, filled her with a regard so strong, so abiding that she joyously answered his every movement with loving ones of her own.

And when he possessed her fully, she clung to him, closing her eyes in the rapture of being his, having him as hers, their bodies meshing in wondrous fulfillment of all she had dreamed for the past few months.

Later, lulled by a symphony of crackling embers, she lay in his arms and knew that no man had ever touched her so tenderly, affected her as deeply as Simon had. It wasn't merely gratitude or lust she felt for him now. It was love. Pure and simple. Her lashes were wet with the knowledge. A tear dropped onto her cheek, but she didn't wipe it away. It was an expressive symbol of this new plane, this new level she had reached with Simon.

He saw it too and watched with fascination the downward slide of the single droplet along her cheek. And just when it was about to touch the soft skin below her ear, he let his tongue taste and savor the salty remembrance of what they had shared.

CHAPTER EIGHT

Adjusting the silver at the table set for two, Joanna stepped back to survey with pride Simon's dining table and the thoroughly romantic atmosphere she'd woven on his behalf with his china, linen and silver. Two attractive candles sat on either side of the centerpiece she'd fashioned with two paper fans and a few silk flowers.

It was to be a feast to tingle the senses. Every one of them, she thought rather smugly, doubting that laundry would be on his mind *this* Thursday evening when he came home to her surprise. Admiring the look of the oriental seafood dish she prepared in his heavy iron wok, Joanna leaned into its aromatic steam to breath deeply. Tantalizing swirls drifted upward, hinting at the bits of lobster and crab meat nestled among the rice— long grain, not instant.

Only the best for Simon, she thought affectionately, smoothing the lines of her dress, a delicately printed silk with mandarin collar. The neckline might be high, but so were the slits at the sides, she reasoned, adjusting the cocktail swizzle sticks in the chignon at the crown of her head.

Glancing at her watch, Joanna returned to the kitchen for the carafe of bubbly chilled wine. He'd be home by seven o'clock as was his habit on Thursdays, after spending the afternoon at the campus library.

Dessert was to be preserved kumquats, simmered in a sweet sauce. She smiled, knowing that Simon would appreciate the exotic fruit even if she couldn't. She'd done everything the way he would have, following the recipes to the letter, washing up as she went, determined to give back at least some of the joy he'd given her the past several days. This surprise for him would be her way of letting him know how much she cared. At five minutes to seven, Joanna lit the candles and sighed with anticipation.

He didn't arrive at seven o'clock.

Nor at eight. At eighty-thirty Joanna snuffed the candles. At nine she ate a peanut-butter sandwich and silently expressed a supreme distaste for rice and anyone who liked it. At nine-thirty she took her third glass of wine into the kitchen where she kicked off her shoes and sat, propping her feet on the adjacent chair. When he turned the lock of the door sometime around ten-thirty, she was still sitting, seething now, her arms crossed in expectation.

"Hi," he said, his jacket tucked beneath his arm as he closed the door and loosened his tie. Simon approached her, a masculine fingertip coaxing her chin up to face him. A discerning gaze moved over her hair, her dress, then dipped to the slit that revealed one thigh. His

144

brows lifted. "My, my, don't you look . . . Eastern."
The tone was deep and husky. Her lips didn't move
when he bent to kiss her. He drew back slightly to offer
a teasing smile. "If not for that peanut butter on your
breath, I'd say you were on the verge of binding your
feet."

She glared at him.

Simon straightened to eye her thoughtfully. "You
look a little pinched, Joanna. You're not having a re-
lapse of the flu, are you?"

"No." She dropped her gaze, resenting his mistaken
concern, resenting the weariness in his face. He didn't
deserve her sympathy. "Where have you been?" she
asked casually, letting irritation bubble inside as he
moved to the sink for a glass of water.

"Tonight was my monthly dinner meeting with Stan
and some of the other department chairmen. Didn't you
know?" The glass went to his lips before he frowned
and lowered it again. "No, I guess you didn't, did you?
Anyway, we meet the sixth of every month."

"The sixth," she said with a nod.

"Stan's lucky number," he offered dryly. "This time
we went to Luigi's. Great pasta there. Very tasty."

"I'm sure it was," she clipped. "Did you have dessert
too?"

"No, the linguine was very filling."

"Ah. So what about your laundry? It *is* Thursday,
you know."

"You bet it is and I intend to get on it right away."
Simon polished off the glass of water before tucking the
empty piece of crystal neatly into the dishwasher. She
hated him for that. Swinging his jacket to rest on his
shoulder, Simon sauntered toward his dining-room

door. "Be back in a minute," he called, pushing against the wood. "I just have to get my—"

Joanna counted three wide swings of the door before he was back in the kitchen again, stopping just inside the room, this time without his jacket. His expression had changed drastically. She reveled in the mild guilt she saw in his face. And the regret. Maybe even a slightly tense embarrassment.

"You made dinner."

Joanna took a sip of wine, room temperature now, and set the goblet carefully back on the table. "Brilliant deduction."

"It looks very . . . tasty too," he offered lamely.

"Is that right?" she demanded coolly. "It looks rather cold to me. Cold and sticky and a little repugnant, actually. Now, four *hours* ago it was fluffy, steamy even, and probably would've been quite tasty. But, as I said, that was four hours ago."

He sighed, combing the awkwardness through the dark strands of his hair. "I'm sorry, Joanna. I know you went to a lot of trouble."

"Yes, I did," she agreed.

"But you should've told me. At least checked my calendar." His palms turned upward with maddening logic. "We could've planned all this."

"I didn't want to plan it," she said evenly. "I wanted to surprise you, Simon. But I'm sure that's an idea that's totally foreign to you."

He blanched at that, every feature tightening in defense. "Wait a minute, Joanna. This is hardly my fault. This meeting is a standing engagement every month. It helps all of us in our teaching. It's routine, but impor-

146

tant. And I'm not going to apologize for being a responsible person or for taking my job seriously."

"God forbid that you should *ever* stray from routine and sobriety," she accused.

Simon stared hard for a moment. Then his anger softened in direct correlation with his voice. "Why don't we have a glass of wine together?" he said, coming closer. "We can still have a nice evening—what's left of it." His hand went to her shoulder to soothe. "What do you say to that?"

She swung a withering stare in his direction. "Kumquats."

His brow furrowed as though she'd spoken in a secret code. "Pardon me?"

"Kumquats." Making the word sound as obscene as she meant it, Joanna went to the refrigerator to remove the glass dessert dish and set it on the table in front of him. "Stuff yourself."

He focused on the fruit halves, now embedded in a cold and gooey sweet sauce. "No, thanks." Then a grating palm went to his jaw. "I said I was sorry, Joanna. My God, what more do you want?"

"What more do I want?" She looked away, shaking her head in disgust, frustration and the knowledge that their relationship hadn't progressed as far as she'd hoped it had. "Let me tell you what I want," she said with miraculous but stinging calm. "I want you to do one thing in your life that hasn't been planned to death first. I want you to do something outrageous one time, Simon. You *need* it badly. Something outrageous without caring what anyone else thinks about it—and don't *touch* me," she warned when he stepped closer to reach out a hand. "And last, but not by any means least, I want you to . . . I'd appreciate it if you would find yourself a nice little cliff somewhere and just jump off, Simon."

Ignoring the wonder in his green eyes, she turned from him. On her way to her own dining room, Joanna silently wished him luck with half a bottle of flat wine, a full basket of dirty laundry and, best of all . . . an empty box of detergent.

By morning her mood had mellowed somewhat, although the disappointment lingered. Joanna had no intention of remaining angry. She hadn't the time or the inclination for power struggles. Knowing her days with Simon were numbered, she only hoped that he realized it too—and that it mattered.

A sleepy yawn accompanied her to the kitchen, where she looked around for telltale signs of last night's confrontation. There were none. She stepped up to Simon's door and pushed it open just enough to peek into the dining room. The dining table had been cleared except for the bright centerpiece of silk flowers and fans.

He must have liked it, she thought, an unwanted but insistent smile teasing her lips. Maybe she shouldn't have used the last of his detergent.

Pushing up the sleeves of her flannel gown, Joanna sighed and moved to the sink to prepare her morning coffee. When she had poured the water into the top of the brewer and set the pot on the burner below, she felt masculine hands slide around her waist to pull her very close. It was Simon. She knew that and silently breathed her delight, her relief.

148

"Hello," she said, maintaining much more calm than she was feeling.

"Aren't you even going to ask who it is?" His tongue flicked over her earlobe.

"I don't have to," she replied casually, but her fingers trembled as she flipped on the brewing switch of the coffee maker. "I'd know that hot tongue anywhere. What are you doing here? I thought you'd be on your way to class by now."

"I'm not going in today. And neither are you. I called in sick an hour ago."

"Oh?" Joanna turned in his embrace and put her hand on his forehead. "You seem fine to me." An understatement if she'd ever made one.

"I'm great," he said slyly, taking her hand to hold it in his. "But I don't think it'll hurt if we miss one day, do you?"

Wriggling free of his grasp, she checked for fever again. "I believe you *are* ill," she teased, but he only smiled, pulling her back into his arms for a tender kiss. It was an action that left her lips alive with a pleasant tingle, reaching deep inside her to alert every nerve ending.

"I want to spend the day with you," he whispered. "No one else."

Her palms went soft against his hard chest. She drew back for a look at his eyes. "What's gotten into you, Simon?"

"You," he said. "How about it, Joanna. Will you call and tell them you can't make it today?"

"Well, I don't know," she hedged, well aware of the gesture he was making. "This is awfully sudden and I—"

"What's the matter," he challenged in sultry tones, "are you so compulsive that you can't do anything spontaneous? Doesn't the spur of the moment excite you?"

If the spur didn't, the big hands moving seductively over her back certainly did. When his lips moved down her neck in taunting nibbles, Joanna drew a broken breath and then groaned. "Just give me a minute to think of a convincing lie. They won't believe we're both sick."

"We're going to make love on the kitchen table," he murmured against her ear.

Her eyes widened, her thoughts becoming amazingly clear. "In that case, my mother's the one who's ill," she stated. "I'll have to go to her immediately, of course. But I'll try my best to be back at Houghton on Monday."

"Good girl."

He'd unfastened the pearl buttons of her gown from throat to waist and slipped a warm palm inside to coax and entice an already willing breast. She clung to the sensuous feel of his nape against her fingers. "Don't you think I should make the call now?"

Simon made no vocal response. When muscular thigh pressed insistently, deliciously, into her, Joanna's voice became high-pitched and breathy. "Do you think they'll have trouble getting substitutes on such short notice?"

"If you're that concerned, I suppose we could put this off for another time," he teased, his breath a zephyr-soft whisper against her bare shoulder.

"Ummm." She smiled a provocative smile. "Not on your Duncan Phyfe."

It was the most exciting experience Joanna had ever

had on a table or any other piece of furniture. During her phone call, he stood beside her, nipping playfully at her ear, nuzzling her breasts, making it very difficult to show the proper concern for her ailing mother. But she managed. When it was done and Simon was pulling her back to the kitchen, Joanna grabbed a few sofa pillows on the way, then followed her heart right into his fascinating fantasy.

She was touched for all time by his passion, his tenderness, his ever-mindful care of her desires, her needs, her comfort. His kisses again filled her with a sense of timelessness, a knowledge that if she could hold him forever, she would. For the first time, the dream attached itself to her heart and refused to let go.

And when he had loved her once more, Joanna clung stubbornly to the dream, knowing all the time that it might not be wise to do so. But wisdom, reason, had no place at all in the love she felt for him.

Simon stood, pulling her up into his arms again. He held her close to him, letting her know that if he was not prepared to give himself completely, there was something . . . *some thing* . . . that drew him irresistibly to her flame . . . the one that blazed bright for him only.

That afternoon he took her to Springfield to see a Western art exhibit at one of the city's museums. As they examined the blue-green hues of a waterfall, Joanna mentioned that a group of her students had invited her for an outing on Sunday at a small, private lake about an hour's drive from Houghton.

When she asked him to go with her, Simon didn't answer, his attention caught by an exquisite bronze sculpture of a gray stallion and colt. She let the matter

151

rest, knowing he'd already made considerable concessions for her.

That evening, they dined in candlelight at last, reheating her seafood rice, which Simon had had the foresight to cover and refrigerate the night before. He showed his sincere appreciation of kumquats by turning the cozy romantic atmosphere into another thrilling show of his affection. She spent a most pleasant night with him, rocked by her own tender dreams, warmed by the circle of his arms.

When he entered the kitchen on Saturday, Joanna observed he was wearing no socks with his shoes. "I haven't had time to do laundry," he explained. "And there's no detergent, anyway. It appears I'm out."

She immediately offered to take care of that problem. But as she made a cup of hot tea for him, Joanna couldn't resist the tease that, since he was out of clean socks, he might also be out of other clothing. Setting his tea on the table, she sidled up to him and dropped a seductive fingertip to his shoulder to taunt. "Just what are you wearing under those jeans?" she asked.

"Nothing." Offering a wry sideways glance before opening the morning paper, he shifted uncomfortably on his chair. "For now, I'll have to 'hang loose,' so to speak."

She smiled with a pretense of shy excitement. "How barbaric, how bohemian, how . . . sexy." Joanna took the newspaper and let it slide to the floor. Pushing him back, she made room for herself on his lap and reached her arms around his neck. "Now, about this libertine attitude you've adopted," she continued in breathless admiration. "It must give you a feeling of such strength, such unharnessed power, such utter emancipation"—

her gaze dropped slyly for a split second—"there, I mean."

He smiled with dry amusement. "Actually it's beginning to feel a bit crowded . . . *there.*"

"Oh, please." Her palm went up to act as a fluttering fan for the counterfeit blush of heat on her face. "Say no more, Simon. Why, I could swoon just thinking about it."

"Could you?" he whispered, beginning to knead and caress her stomach. His mouth pressed into the thin silk that covered her breasts, searing the soft skin beneath. "Try to control yourself, Joanna. I want you to be fully conscious for what's going to happen to you."

There was no pretense at all in the shallow breaths she drew in and expelled. She opened her mouth, then quickly closed it, licking her lips as one shoulder lifted in the slightest shrug. "If you insist."

He did insist—and made her very glad she remained awake through the entire demonstration. Again laundry was forgotten until evening, when she helped him separate whites from colors and took great pleasure in folding clothes with Simon.

In the morning they shared the Sunday newspaper in bed. She concentrated on "Dear Abby" and the horoscope, while he devoured the editorial page. Then they exchanged their sections and afterward debated the fine points of the opinions presented. Moving on to the funnies, Simon read "Peanuts" aloud while Joanna, peering over his shoulder, provided a running commentary of the *true* relationship between Lucy and Charlie Brown.

Later she dressed warmly in thermal underwear beneath her plaid flannel shirt and jeans in preparation for the cookout with her students. Stuffing her hair into a knit stocking cap, she reached for her thick wool socks. She was just pulling on a new pair of hiking boots when Simon entered the bedroom.

"Ready to go?" he asked.

She looked up from her lacing, a little surprised to see him wrapped in a fur-lined parka, holding a pair of gloves. "Almost," she replied, conscious of the faint hope that trickled cautiously through her.

"Mind if I come along?"

Her mouth melted into a tender smile. "I'd love it."

"Well," he said with a shrug, "I'm probably going to hate it but, God help me, I think I'm getting used to you."

"Oh, Simon," she said with a teasing shake of her head. "Do you know how dangerous it is to be confessing things like that?"

"Yes, I think I do." His eyes twinkled a mysterious gratitude. "But I can't seem to help it, Joanna." He took hold of her stocking cap and yanked it down to cover her eyes. "Until you came along, I never knew what Lucy *really* thought about old Charlie Brown."

The Missouri air was nippy and sweet, laced with the pungent smell of burning hickory. What had begun as a brisk, invigorating tramp through the woods had ended in friendly chatter and chili around the campfire. Joanna was glad for the invitation to spend the day with her students this way. She was even more pleased that Simon had come with her to share in the fun.

He seemed a bit reluctant to get too close to her today, but Joanna attributed that to the presence of other people. He'd made it clear that he wasn't altogether resigned to hobnobbing with students from Houghton.

She, on the other hand, felt quite comfortable in the casual atmosphere with the three young men and as many young women. Joanna enjoyed hearing them talk about their college experiences and even shared some of her own when they expressed interest in hearing about campus life in the "old days."

"To be honest," she said, stirring her spoon in the Styrofoam cup of chili, "I'm a little concerned about the complacency I see on campuses today. When I was in college we were more involved in issues. There was always some kind of demonstration going on." She shrugged. "At least it seemed that way."

Out of the corner of her eye, Joanna didn't miss Simon's instant hard focus on the patch of ground between his boots a few feet away from her.

Liz Mathison, one of Joanna's more philosophical students, pushed horn-rimmed glasses back to her nose and frowned. "I've been rather concerned about that myself," she said. "About student indifference, I mean. What kinds of things did you protest?"

Joanna smiled in remembrance. "Anything and everything," she admitted wryly. "The Vietnam War was very important to everyone, of course, along with poverty and the draft. But our causes weren't always so noble. Once a group of us staged a feisty demonstration over some parking tickets we got for using the faculty parking lot." Placing the back of one palm to her forehead in feigned drama, she closed her eyes in lament. "There was nothing too small or too insignificant to escape our wrath."

Laughter erupted around the fire, then gradually faded again. "God, it must've been exciting . . . to get belligerent over a parking ticket." Alan Potter downed the last of his soda before husky shoulders lifted in a sigh.

"Yes, well, don't go right out and burn your driver's license," Simon admonished dryly, still staring at the ground. "It was exciting sometimes, but it was also a waste of energy at other times. These days students have more important things to worry about than where to park their cars."

"Right," David Cullen, a pre-law student said. "Such as how we're going to compete in an already over-crowded job market."

His wife Rosalyn's almond-shaped eyes came alive with encouragement. "And how a couple just starting out can find an affordable place to live," she added, stroking the sleeve of David's jacket.

Willie Vincent nodded. "And then there's the hassle of getting the old man to lay out the cash for stereo speakers."

"Oh, yeah, that's a world problem that's preyed on my mind a lot lately," Alan jeered, shaking his blond head in wonder. "Comments like that are just more evidence that we're part of the 'me' generation. Sometimes I feel like we ought to be doing more for others." The confession brought a dissatisfied twist to one corner of his mouth. He dipped into the cast-iron kettle for more chili.

Joanna certainly hadn't meant to bring an air of sobriety to the gathering. This was supposed to be a sort of last hurrah for her students before next week's finals. "If you want something changed, you have to be willing to speak up loud and clear," she said at last, and then ignored the mild accusation in Simon's eyes. "This chili is delicious." Spooning another bite from the cup to her

156

mouth, she licked her lips and smiled. "I might have to stay on at Houghton permanently if I can count on being invited to these affairs often."

"Have you considered that?" Alan asked. "Houghton needs more professors like you."

"Why, thank you, Alan. It's so nice of you to say that."

A few other students echoed the compliment. Joanna found herself caught up in the fervor. "Well, I've always wanted to start a community consumer program. What better way than to have it sponsored by a college like Houghton? In addition to teaching in the regular curriculum, of course."

"Yeah!"

"That's a great idea," someone said. "We could really get some things done with you here, Dr. Sinclair."

Wondering what *things* they had in mind, Joanna smiled, well aware that Simon sat very still and silent.

Alan voiced the question she herself longed to ask. "Dr. Gregory, what do you think about Dr. Sinclair staying on?"

Only then did Joanna turn to Simon. "Yes, Dr. Gregory. Why don't you tell us all the reasons why this is an irrational and totally untenable idea?" she teased, and then watched his serious expression turn even more thoughtful.

He brought his knees farther up to rest his elbows on them. "The idea itself isn't a bad one. But right now I don't think it would stand a chance with the board. You have to remember that Richard—the other Dr. Sinclair —will be back next fall. And Houghton has only so many slots for the department."

"Are you saying there isn't room for another good

157

economics instructor at Houghton?" It was Alan, show-ing his usual bravado. "I think that's absurd."

Simon's face went grim as he placed the empty cup and spoon on a relatively flat rock. "Absurd or not, these days the college is cutting back on expenditures. It has enough trouble just keeping up with the latest tech-nological equipment. I don't think there's room in the budget for another professor—not in my department anyway. Unless, of course, Dr. Sinclair were to take someone else's job. Mine, for instance."

"Oh, no," Rosalyn spoke up. "That's not what we want."

"Thank you." Simon tipped his head in a dry, but courtly, gesture.

"Couldn't you put in a good word for her with the Dean of Instruction or someone?" Alan persisted.

Again Simon was patient. "I could. But as I said, I doubt it would do any good." Then he turned a deep, caressing tone to Joanna. "You understand."

She certainly did. But now that the idea had been planted firmly in her mind, Joanna wanted very much to pursue it. A chance to remain here, a chance to be with Simon to give their relationship time to grow. How could she not pursue it? She resolved to speak to Frank Patterson at the first opportunity. The Dean of Instruc-tion might not be as pessimistic as Simon appeared to be.

"All I know is that Dr. Sinclair gets my vote," Willie piped. "For all that's worth," he added good-naturedly. "We students don't have a lot of influence in the budget at Houghton."

"Yeah, well it doesn't necessarily have to stay that

way." Alan stood up. "In the meantime, I'm ready for some serious fishing."

Others rose in agreement. The group gradually split up. Most headed toward the heated dock while Rosalyn and David wandered in the direction of an old tire swing that was suspended from a sturdy tree branch. Joanna was left alone at the fire with Simon.

When he stood and came toward her, she scooted aside to share her rock with him. "You do understand, don't you?" he whispered, concern crinkling the corners of his eyes.

"Yes." She smiled, comprehending perfectly the man's usual caution with any new idea.

"It's true that we can always use good instructors," he said, taking her hand in his to warm it. It worked beautifully. "But it just isn't in the cards—not in the next few years, anyway."

"There's no need to explain, Simon." Squeezing the masculine fingers that entwined hers, Joanna reached up to kiss him, letting her lips convey the tenderness, the love, she felt for him.

He savored the message, giving back one of his own in the process before releasing her to push himself to his feet. "If I stay here much longer, I could make a complete spectacle of myself," he said grimly, his breathing markedly quickened. "And I'd rather do that in more private surroundings. I'm going for a walk, Joanna. Let me know when you're ready to start for home."

Home. The word had a very nice ring to it. He took the cliff path and Joanna watched him until his alluring shoulders had disappeared into the brush. Then, pulling her heavy jacket tighter against the chill, she looked toward the lake and the blazing sunset beyond. Since

159

the ill-fated dinner, he'd been absolutely wonderful to her. She could hardly believe that her anger had moved him to such dramatic—not to mention romantic—responses. He was trying hard to please her. Now Joanna felt almost guilty for the things she'd said. But not so guilty as to take them back. Apparently, he'd viewed every one of her accusations as a personal challenge.

Sighing with satisfaction, she pulled her knit hat farther down over her ears. His insistence that they call in sick had been quite impulsive for a duty-bound man like Simon, she reasoned. And as for doing something outrageous, well . . . she had to admit that making love on the breakfast table was one of the more outrageous things she herself had ever accomplished. She could've died with love for him that day. Ummm. But what a way to go, she mused. He'd turned all her sarcastic comments into brilliantly executed, never-to-be-forgotten memories.

Slipping on her wool gloves, Joanna caught sight of him standing at the edge of the cliff above her. When she waved her affection, he answered with a waving gesture of his own, then put his hands into the back pockets of his jeans. She tried to remember the last bitter thing she'd said to him that frustrating evening. Oh, yes, she thought with a smile. She'd told him to jump off a cliff. It seemed such a childish outburst now that she had some distance from it.

But as Joanna watched him, his pensive stare moving over the water some ten to fifteen feet below him, her smile slowly began to fade, replaced by a doubting frown. When he moved even closer to the edge, her muscles tensed suddenly. She swallowed. He wouldn't do that, she thought, stubbornly casting the silly fear

160

aside. But her smile was nervous this time. The doubt returned, becoming stronger with each moment he remained up there where she couldn't touch him.

"Simon," she whispered helplessly.

All the way up the path, she denied that he would do such a thing, angry with herself for even thinking it, angry that she'd ever said it. But she hadn't *meant* it, for God's sake. No one in his right mind would jump off a cliff in the middle of December just to prove a point. Especially Simon, she assured herself, pushing overhanging branches out of her way in a now desperate urge to get to him before he did something crazy. Was this why he'd insisted on coming with her to the lake?

The uphill climb was stealing both her breath and her ability to think clearly. She forced herself to move faster, even though she still refused to fully accept the need for it.

At last in the clearing, she saw him, his back to her as he craned out over the edge.

"Simon—my God—don't jump!"

His startled backward glance was a frown. "Jump? Are you crazy?"

But she was already moving toward him. As he turned around, Joanna tripped on an exposed tree root and fell into him, knocking him off balance.

Time seemed to stop as, clinging to each other, they teetered precariously at the cliff's edge. Joanna looked up and inwardly cringed at the resigned disgust she saw in his green eyes. He shook his head, very slowly it seemed, his mouth a tight line of regret.

"Well, Goddamn," he muttered, toppling over the precipice, taking her with him as he went.

CHAPTER NINE

As though in defiance of the surrounding darkness, the headlights on the station wagon beamed a steady patch of light along the highway. Chilled despite the continual blast of hot air from the heater and the blanket around her, Joanna kept her gaze on the center line, risking a glance at Simon only now and then when her courage would allow it. His tight fists remained wrapped around the steering wheel. He said nothing. But his every shiver offered her a grim reminder of being dragged coughing and sputtering from the icy water.

She'd never seen him so angry. She doubted he'd ever *been* so angry. Still he'd managed to keep it from the students. Even when Willie mentioned what a great cartoon the scene would make for the campus newspaper, Simon had merely stared in silence at the ground. Fortunately, no one had laughed. But when Willie went on to suggest a caption, *Head of Economics falls for visiting instructor,* Simon's jaw had tightened to something akin to rage. He'd suggested—strongly—that they leave for home immediately. She had agreed.

Her bare feet had begun to thaw and she wriggled her toes to encourage the circulation. She'd apologized—profusely. So far, though, Simon had not deigned to discuss it. She could only hope he would feel better with dry clothes, hot tea and precious distance between them.

His phone was ringing when they entered the kitchen. While he went to answer it, Joanna put water on to boil for him, then made herself a pot of coffee. When Simon returned a few minutes later, his face was flushed even more.

"Bad news?" she asked lamely.

"Oh, no," he said, his sarcasm biting into her cheeks. "It was President Brandt. He just wanted to say that he hoped I was feeling better and that we enjoyed our trip to the museum on Friday—he was certain it was more pleasant than spending a boring day in the classroom." Simon wrenched a chair from the table and sat down to unlace his soggy, squeaking boots. "Just his clever way of letting me know that I didn't get away with anything."

She drew a deep breath and let it out again with a small shrug. "I guess it was rather stupid—going out in public like that?"

It was the wrong thing to say. Joanna knew it the moment his gaze lifted from the boots to pierce her already weakened confidence. "I'm not acquainted with the fine points of lying to satisfy ridiculous impulses," he said through gritted teeth. "Perhaps I should've consulted you on the right way to handle it."

Her chin shot up, but Joanna consciously forced her

mouth to remain closed. He was blaming her now, but with time he would see things differently. She knew that. When he calmed down and thought about it he would realize that a few unfortunate incidents shouldn't negate all the wonderful times they'd spent together. And so, despite her own anger, she didn't allow herself to voice the flaming response that formed in her mind just then. Turning away from the tempting words that hovered dangerously on her lips, she went instead to change out of her own wet clothes, hoping he damn well appreciated her restraint.

Two days passed before Simon smiled again. Even then the effort wasn't what Joanna could call genuine. The episode at the lake became one of the more amusing subjects of conversation on campus. Students and faculty alike seemed to look upon both her and Simon in a new, more familiar light.

Stan Farber was merciless, never missing a chance to joke about their accident. "Picture this," he said, spreading his palms for the imagined panorama. "A new event in the summer Olympics—*pairs* in platform diving. Go for the gold, you two."

Joanna took the teasing in stride. To her it was nothing more than friends taking the opportunity to laugh about something. Considering that her own supply of amusement had dropped to a dangerous low, she understood.

Not so for Simon. He denied—vigorously—that it bothered him. Nonetheless, she sensed that his new notoriety disagreed fiercely with the image he'd enjoyed before—the one of a responsible, practical and intensely private man.

For Joanna, the week passed rockily despite all her

attempts to smooth over the strain between them. She was plagued with the knowledge that time was running out. The end of her semester at Houghton was painfully near. Finals were already in progress. Simon was preoccupied with campus duties, but even when he relaxed at home, he seemed troubled, even distant at times.

He made love to her once. The moments in his arms were as physically satisfying as ever, but she felt his emotional detachment—as though he knew their relationship was about to end and was preparing for the loss. He could love, but he wouldn't allow himself to feel too deeply. He skillfully sidestepped all talk of the future. Aware that he must be thinking a lot about their relationship and its effect on him, both personally and professionally, she knew no way to convince him that it was right. That it was good. That it would work.

Helpless to stop his withdrawal from her, Joanna reverted to a heretofore tried-and-true rationalization. Once she'd been very adept at convincing herself that whatever she couldn't have, she really didn't want in the first place. But this time her old trick didn't work. This time she wanted Simon. And the wanting wouldn't go away.

On Friday her eyes were open long before her alarm went off. After a harrowing week, she'd planned to sleep in since the final exam for her consumer finance class was scheduled for ten thirty. But her sleep had been restless, fitful, and by eight o'clock she was dressed and sipping her second cup of coffee.

It was time to think of leaving, she knew. Her talk with Dean Patterson a few days earlier had offered little hope for staying on at Houghton. Still he had agreed to make the recommendation on her behalf this morning in a meeting with President Brandt. Simon would be there too, as would all department chairmen, to discuss preliminary plans for next year's budget. She couldn't help wondering if he would speak up for her.

When the ringing of the phone intruded upon her thoughts, Joanna took her coffee to the living room and lifted the receiver.

"Hello."

"Joanna, it's Simon. I want you to get over here right away."

She frowned at the tightness of his tone. "My first class isn't—"

"Just get here."

The click of the phone severing the connection jarred her a little. He was angry. And apparently she was the cause of that anger. Reaching for her handbag and briefcase, Joanna sighed, knowing it seemed to be par for the course lately.

As she swung the El Camino into the faculty parking lot a few minutes later, Joanna was aware of the crowd outside the Administration Building. At first glance she saw nothing unusual in that. Students often gathered at various places on campus between classes. But a closer look as she neared the entrance to the Business Building next door halted her steps for a moment. The crowd was too organized for casual conversation. She caught sight of a few placards, not quite legible at that distance, then heard the chanting.

Joanna frowned. A demonstration at Houghton? Stepping off the sidewalk and onto the grass, she decided to investigate this intriguing phenomenon. Was this the reason for Simon's anger? What did it have to do with her? Pressing closer into the throng, she saw with startling clarity what it had to do with her.

Many of the faces were known to Joanna. Several of her students offered enthusiastic greetings. But she was hardly aware of that. Her gaze fastened with alarm on a placard, one indicating that the college budget was *everyone's* business. And then on the one that said students were consumers too. Alan Potter was holding that particular sign. He broke from the line of protesters to walk toward her.

"Hi, Dr. Sinclair," he called. "We were hoping you'd come out to support us." Then he smiled knowingly. "Does it bring back memories?"

"Oh, Alan," she breathed, "what are you doing?"

"We're becoming involved, just like you did," he said with none-too-subdued pride, his heavy jacket making him look a lot like a gentle bear.

"That's—very nice, but . . . do you think this is the right way?" she asked.

"You know what they say"—Alan lifted his sign a little higher—"all's fair in love and war."

"I wonder." Joanna's smile was grim as she acknowledged so *many* familiar faces around her. She sensed that the next several minutes, perhaps more, weren't going to be fair at all. "I'll talk to you later, Alan. I need to see a man about a muzzle."

Simon was standing at the window when she entered his second-floor office. Joanna was very tempted to leave him that way. She dreaded the angry connection she knew he had already made between her and the demonstration outside.

"Simon, I'm here," she announced, gathering her innocence around her. "But aren't you supposed to be at a meeting with President Brandt?"

"I was," he said, his voice amazingly calm. Still he didn't turn from the window. "We had a slight interruption and had to postpone the meeting."

"Oh?" She edged farther into the room. "Anything serious?"

"Yes, I think you could say that," he drawled, but now she noticed white knuckles pressed against the wide window sash. "Just after we got started, about fifteen students burst into the room and refused to leave."

"Oh, no." Joanna had a sickening feeling that those students might be part of the group she'd seen outside. "What did they want?"

"A say in next year's budget. 'Student input,' I believe is the way it was phrased. And of course they wanted to make sure you were hired on a permanent basis. Even called themselves *Sinclair's Raiders.*"

She nodded numbly, then lifted her gaze to the ceiling. "How quaint. But I'm sure they thought they were helping my cause." Joanna glanced dryly at Simon, his broad back stiff with stubbornness. "Well, tell me. Were they successful?"

Only then did he turn to her, disgust pinching the corner of his mouth. "Frank Patterson never had a chance. You've been turned down for a permanent teaching position."

At that moment she was oddly relieved. But before she could give it much thought, he was motioning her to his side. "Come here, Joanna. I assume you've noticed the *event* taking place in front of the Administration Building." He waited until she had reluctantly

168

taken the steps to the window. "Notice anything familiar about the people down there?"

"I'm aware that some of them are my students," she admitted tightly. "But I—"

"All of them, Joanna. Every one with a sign is a student of yours," he observed dryly. "Unfortunately some of them are also my students. And as chairman of the Economics Department, the responsibility for the disruption of the meeting and that little demonstration out there somehow falls on my shoulders."

She looked up in surprise and irritation. "Why that's ridiculous. You didn't know this was going to happen."

"No, I didn't." Then his gaze swung pointedly down to her. "Did you?"

Drawing a deep and angry breath, Joanna returned his stare. "Of course I didn't know."

He turned back to the window as though he didn't quite believe her. "I've been at Houghton for four years now," he said evenly. "And I've never seen anything like this. I hoped when you were hired that you wouldn't bring this kind of atmosphere with you. What did you say to them?"

"I'm not involved in this, Simon. I might've said a few things—I really don't remember *what* I said. But I certainly never suggested that they disrupt your meeting with President Brandt." She moved away, but he followed.

"Don't you know how much they respect your opinion? What they would do for your approval? Hell, you're a celebrity here. Your name alone could send them running for their Magic Markers." He was beginning to rant.

Joanna turned to him, her heavy sigh giving him

pause. "I think you're taking this much too seriously, Simon. So a few students are demonstrating against the administration's policies. It isn't the end of the world. Why shouldn't they have their say? This isn't the Dark Ages."

"This isn't a democracy, either, Joanna. This is a conservative, private college. And like it or not, instructors —temporary or otherwise—are expected to support the administration's policies—however medieval they may appear." He came closer. She saw the anger in his face, anger that was directed at her. "In a few days, you, like the proverbial hare, will be leaving," he said. "But I, like the *dull* but steady tortoise, will be plodding along in the job I was hired to do."

It was true. She would be leaving. Very soon. But this wasn't the time to think about that. There was much more to this than demonstrations or disruptions. She knew that now. She only wished he could admit the most disappointing fact. "Do you want me to talk to the students?" she asked. "I'm open to anything."

"You're *open* to *every*thing," he accused. "But I wonder if you really ever *think* about anything. Anyway, it's a little late for you to behave responsibly, don't you think?"

"What I think is that you're making a mountain out of a molehill, Simon. More to the point, a case against *us,* you and me, out of some trumped-up rationalization. Why don't you admit that it's our relationship that's really bothering you. Why don't you admit that you're embarrassed to show how you really—"

"Don't you understand?" he demanded harshly, taking hold of her arms to jerk her toward him. "Since you've been here I've done things I've never—" He stopped suddenly and then, more slowly, let his hands slide from her, leaving her strangely longing to feel his touch again. He lifted a restless palm to rub the back of his neck before he went on. "What happens between us in private is one thing. My God, that in *itself* is crazy enough. But when it affects our professional lives, it's time to stop and think about a few things."

"All *right.*" Knowing her voice was shaking, Joanna struggled to regain control of it. Struggled to calm her ragged breathing. "I'm sorry if I've embarrassed you, Simon. I'm sorry if you feel I've jeopardized your position at Houghton. But I'll be damned if I'll apologize for—for—what we've shared these past few months." The words and their meaning brought a sudden weakness to her limbs. Joanna looked away. There didn't seem to be much point in further discussion. Reaching for her handbag, she turned to him once more. He was facing the window again. He didn't want to look at her. But he would listen . . . one more time.

"I've been good for you, Simon. And you've been good for me," she said quietly. "I know that. And nothing you can say or do will ever make me believe differently."

Somehow Joanna finished up her last day at Houghton. Then she went home to get her class records in order and pack. It was late in the evening when she stood at his dining-room door. She thought about knocking. She even lifted a fist to the wood before it occurred to her that she hadn't done that in a very long time. Lowering her hand, she refused to do it now, refused to go back to the time when he'd expected it of her.

171

Opening the door, she moved in the shadows toward the living room. A single lamp behind him splashed light past Simon's shoulder onto the book he was reading.

She hesitated, dreading the last encounter, needing to stop and look at him just once more, sitting in his recliner . . . the way she had seen him many times. Times when she had joined him there and loved him. Both the memory and the reality caught helplessly in her throat, but she swallowed the feeling and moved closer to him. He was frowning, perhaps unconsciously, the creases deep in his forehead. She denied the impulse to approach and caress the strain from his face.

Simon looked up, cutting short her covert observation. The creases disappeared from his face but the tightness remained. He brought the recliner forward to an upright position. "Sit down, Joanna." His voice was deep and hoarse as though from lack of use. Clearing his throat, he motioned to the sofa.

She didn't want to sit. She couldn't face the pretense of coziness with him. Not now. It would be such a lie when she felt his distance, his tension. Hers too. Joanna remained standing behind the sofa, allowing her fingers to stroke the soft material of the slipcover in search of comfort. A question formed in his brows and she sighed.

"I'm all packed, Simon. I'll be leaving in the morning."

He seemed rather surprised at that. "Tomorrow?" He rose from the chair where she wished he would stay. She didn't want to see his hands go into his pockets. It was too endearing. Too undeniably Simon. But they did. "I thought you'd wait until Monday," he said. "I didn't

172

think you'd be able to get the grades posted before then."

"The records are all in order," she said quietly. "I talked with President Brandt a little while ago and told him that I need to be in Tulsa on Monday. He agreed and said I could leave the grades with you."

Simon nodded, moving slowly toward the bar. "And *do* you need to be in Tulsa on Monday?"

Joanna looked down at the sofa. Her fingers had begun to frantically rub its fabric. She forced them to stop. "Yes, I think I do."

After a moment, she heard the clink of ice against glass. "Would you like a drink?" he asked.

She shook her head. "None for me, thanks."

Simon recapped the bottle of bourbon. Leaving the pair of glasses on the bar, he walked back to his chair. But he didn't sit. Please sit, she silently begged. Still, he didn't. Reluctantly Joanna came around to perch on the arm of the sofa.

"Richard will be coming back on Sunday," he said, finally lowering himself to the recliner. "He'll be sorry he missed you."

Richard. She wished she could see him now. She needed to see him. He would help her through this. Help her to put the disappointment into some kind of perspective. Joanna drew a deep breath. "I'll see him at Christmas."

"What about your water bed?" Simon asked. "I could—"

"It's dismantled and ready to go. I'll load everything in the morning." Why was he doing this when it only prolonged the pain? She didn't know how long she could endure the casual chitchat.

"I'll help you with the cans." The tender smile he offered was very nearly her undoing. "I remember the day you arrived," he said. "My day lilies will never be the same."

Her mouth trembled with unspoken regret. Nor will I, Simon. Nor will I. He had no right to ask her to smile at the memories now. It was too soon for that. It would be a long time before she could do that. She would cry if he didn't stop.

Joanna stood up. "Simon, I have a few things to do. Some phone calls to make." God, when had she become so courteous, so polite with him? "If I don't see you in the morning—I'll leave my class records in the kitchen." The moment had come and she didn't know what to say, how to handle it. Or even whether she could handle it. Now he was standing too, staring, waiting. "Thank you for—everything, Simon. You've made my—time at Houghton very—" Her gaze slid helplessly to the floor. "I'm sorry if I caused—" Joanna shook her head, her mouth quivering with the triteness, the utter nonsense of what she was saying when her thoughts, her love, ran so much deeper.

A gentle masculine fingertip lifted her chin to face him. Green eyes reflected her own regret. His kiss was a feather-light touch on her lips, fleeting, and yet she knew she would always be warmed by the memory of it.

Drawing away, Simon went back to sit in his chair. "Joanna," he said, his voice now tight with restraint. "I've never been very romantic." He shrugged as though resigned to that. "I guess I'm not the type. But you must know how much I care for you. It's just that I'm not ready for—something permanent. Not now." He looked up, his eyes pleading for understanding.

"Maybe I never will be. And it isn't fair to offer less . . . not to you."

She wanted to argue. She wanted to say he was very romantic. That she didn't care about what was fair. That she only cared about him. But she said none of it. Because she sensed that he wouldn't want her to.

"Okay." The word choked forth on a fragile breath. Joanna walked to the door, but something made her turn back one more time to face him. Get up, Simon, she silently begged. Get up. Get up and surprise me. Just once more. Please.

But he didn't. She smiled, her eyes stinging with the gathering tears. She had known he wouldn't surprise her. Not anymore. He wouldn't even look at her. But he was wrong, she thought stubbornly. He was full of romance. For a time he'd shared it with her. She had seen it. Felt it. She knew it existed. Why else would her heart be breaking so irreparably now?

"Good-bye, Simon." The words were a whisper. She wasn't even sure that he heard.

Simon did hear. As he watched her leave, his hand lifted to stop her. But slowly he brought it back to his side. It wouldn't be right to do that when he didn't know. When he wasn't sure. But God, at this moment he loved her.

CHAPTER TEN

Attaching another glass ornament to a branch of the Scotch pine, Joanna silently reiterated that she wasn't in the mood for decorating the Christmas tree Richard had brought. This Christmas Eve she'd planned to forgo the holiday trappings. Had told him that very plan on the phone the day before. But when he'd appeared on her doorstep that morning offering the rather skinny tree in exchange for a "decent" lunch, there didn't seem to be much choice but to drape the pathetic specimen with some kind of Christmas dignity.

In any case, she was always glad for a visit from her older brother, but especially now when his friendly face, his comforting presence, meant even more. He'd stopped by on his way to their mother's place in Muskogee. Having already strung the lights around the tree, he sat now, ensconced at one end of the sofa to peruse the morning newspaper. So far he'd said nothing about Simon or Springfield, but the omission itself was revealing. He was too perceptive to miss the strain in her face, too loving to nag her about it.

As she bent to the old steamer trunk to pick and choose among the antique ornaments that had been part of her legacy from Granny, Joanna glanced now and then toward Richard. He looked very much like her, she supposed, except that his eyes were bluer, his face more angular, his hair a warmer brown. And now that he'd been to Florida, his skin was darker. He was taller, too. But there were more than physical differences. He was more disciplined. More persevering. More orderly. Richard was more everything.

"How came you to be so perfect, Richard?" she asked casually. It wasn't the first time, either. The question was the beginning of a favorite game they'd played as children.

He didn't look up from the paper. "A charmed life, I suppose. Or maybe clean living. How came you to be so sad?"

She frowned. That wasn't the way it went. He was supposed to ask *How came you to be so clever?* "I'm not sad," she defended. "Who could be sad at Christmastime? Especially when I know you've bought me a wonderful present. You did buy me a wonderful present, didn't you?"

"Well, a present, anyway. You know you're just as good as ever at changing the subject."

"I'm not—"

"You haven't said much about your semester at Houghton. Was it the satisfying experience you hoped it would be?"

"Yes, for the most part."

"Is teaching something you'd like to continue?"

177

She swallowed. "Probably not. I've always liked lecturing and writing, Richard. I'm more suited to it I think, setting my own hours, my own routine. Although I did appreciate the chance to teach for a semester. I learned a lot myself. Now that I've done it though, I realize it's not for me." She attached her favorite glass bulb to one of the higher branches of the tree, then reached for another one. "So, how did you like coming back to snowy Springfield after being spoiled by the Florida sun?"

"You mean before or after I put my bed back together?"

Joanna's glance was sheepish. "Sorry. I took yours down to make room for mine. Then I sort of left in a hurry."

"Why was that?"

"Oh, I don't know. It was the last day of the semester. I'd been thinking about coming home. All of a sudden the mood hit me and"—Joanna shrugged—"you know me when a mood hits."

He didn't believe her. Joanna could tell by his silence. Still, after a moment Richard nodded gallantly. "And Simon. How did you two get along? Was he helpful?"

He was wonderful. Simon was wonderful, she breathed helplessly. "He was—very nice to me." She had wanted to share her sorrow with someone. Had planned to do that with Richard. But now Joanna found that she couldn't. Maybe it was too soon—no more than a week had passed since she'd left Springfield. Or maybe it was just too personal, too sensitive a subject to share with anyone, even a brother as understanding as hers had always been. "How is he, Richard?"

"Simon?" Richard frowned thoughtfully. "I'd say

178

he's a little grumpy these days. Testy might be a better word."

Joanna turned back to the tree and clutched a box of tinsel. "How's that?"

"Well, I went in to do my laundry last Monday—the way I always do on Monday—and he practically snapped my head off. Told me there was something detestable about people who got too set in their ways."

"Really?" she asked, her tone as nonchalant as she could make it.

"Yes, he also said that there were a hell of a lot more exciting things to do than laundry for a man my age."

Trembling fingers lifted a strand of silver to the tree. Joanna draped it over a spray of pine needles, then stepped back pressing her palms together to hide the quiver of pain. "Well, everyone has bad days, I suppose."

"Maybe. He seemed to know what he was talking about, Joanna."

"Come and put the star on the tree, Richard—please," she added weakly.

He mercifully got up to grant her request. "You're not going to tell me what happened, are you?" It was more statement than question as he took the delicate ornament from her.

Joanna stared into her brother's eyes, hoping to convey the plea. "No," she said quietly, shaking her head as she looked away. "Not yet, Richard. Maybe never."

"Well, it couldn't have been too bad. After all, you didn't paint my bathroom."

She smiled despite the damnable tears that gathered threateningly in her eyes. "I controlled myself."

"Did Simon?"

She nodded. "Oh, yes. Simon was the soul of restraint." Turning away, Joanna took a deep, soothing breath into her lungs and then shrugged. "Granny always said no man would have me the way I was." She felt the firm comfort of Richard's hands on her shoulders.

"Joanna, you know she was joking. I think she always envied you," he whispered. "I know she left you the things she prized most—all her books, her essays, her poems, all came in that old steamer trunk." He dropped a kiss on the top of her head. "You know what I think? I think any man who doesn't think my sister is wonderful is a stupid fool."

"Richard, please . . ." She moved away, closing the lid of the trunk, hoping to put an end to the subject and the tension in her throat. "Thank you for the tree, brother dear," and the kindness, she added silently. "It'll be beautiful this evening when the lights are on. What shall we do now?"

But he was already reaching for his coat on the back of the sofa. "I think I'll be on my way to mother's. Sure you won't come with me?"

"No, I'm going to stay here tonight. I have some things to do."

He looked at the clutter of gift boxes, sheets of bright-colored wrapping paper and ribbon strewn haphazardly on the carpet around the tree. "I can see that."

"When you arrived, I was wrapping your present," she said in defense.

"In that case, who am I to criticize a little clutter?"

Walking him into the hallway, she reached up to hug him, clinging with gratitude for the understanding he had offered. "Tell mother I'll be in Muskogee first thing

180

in the morning," she said, and then watched him amble slowly down the sidewalk.

The knock came sometime after midnight. Frowning, Joanna balanced her paintbrush on the edge of the can and tiptoed warily into the living room. "Who is it?" There was no answer to her faint, cautious whisper. She cleared her throat. "Who is it?" she demanded in her most surly voice.

"I love you."

"What?" The distant masculine voice made her heart begin to pound. Oh, my God, a pervert on Christmas Eve! "Go away, you—"

"Joanna, it's Simon. I love you."

"Simon?" A picture of herself in jeans and the paint-splattered sweat shirt sent her hands to her hair to make quick swipes at the tangles. Seeing the futility in that, she unlocked the door and flung it open to find him relaxed against the door casing. "Simon, what are you *doing* here?"

"I . . . love you," he said with a shrug.

Joanna couldn't speak. She could only look at the man who'd finally said the words. The sensuous mouth, the tousled hair, the attractive frame that had come all the way from Springfield. God, she loved him too. She took hold of a woolly brown sleeve and pulled him inside.

His eyes held a look of determination, tinged with apprehension. "Well, that didn't seem to impress you much. Let me begin again. I got hungry, Joanna. I've driven all this way for a peanut-butter sandwich. I heard you make the best."

"You're lying," she said breathily.

181

"Yes, I am," he confessed dryly. "But what tipped you off?"

She smiled the delight that filtered softly through her. "You don't like peanut butter."

"I'd be willing to learn." Simon offered the heavy jacket he carried and let Joanna hang it on the coat tree. "Didn't the part about hearing that you made the best bother you any?"

"Not at all," she said with a smug shake of her head. "That's already been well established."

"Oh." His gaze roamed past her to the clutter of the living room. "Did you have some sort of party here tonight?"

"No, just me." She turned to walk into the midst of crossword-puzzle books, magazines, a jigsaw puzzle, its pieces scattered across a sheet of posterboard. "I didn't quite know what to do with myself on Christmas Eve, so I guess I just did everything." Her nerves were suddenly strung taut. Not knowing quite what to do now either, she bent to scoop the *National Geographic* from the carpet.

"Later, Joanna." Simon was behind her, reaching around to take the magazine and toss it to the coffee table. "Let me say what I came to say before I lose my nerve."

When he took hold of her shoulders and turned her to him, she knew that neatness didn't count. Not now. Her mouth opened to say "All right," but no sound would come from her lips. And so she closed them again, staring up into warm green eyes.

"I—" Simon broke off with a groan, pulling her to him as his mouth settled sweetly on hers. His masculine scent enveloped her, luring her arms up to encircle his neck. His tongue moved over her lips in possessive hunger and she couldn't seem to think clearly anymore. She could only feel. Letting the heady enchantment surround her, Joanna clung to him even when he drew his lips from hers.

"I love you," he said, and made certain this time she heard and felt his declaration.

"Oh, Simon, are you sure?" She wanted no doubts, no reservations.

"As sure as any man can be when he's under that kind of influence." He led her to the sofa and with gentle pressure lowered her to the cushions, where he joined her. Resting an arm along the edge of the tuxedo back, he leaned very close. "I don't believe that anyone has ever made me feel as vulnerable as you have, Joanna. It scared the hell out of me. I'd promised myself that after Susan, I'd never feel that way again. I sensed from the beginning that you and I couldn't have a casual affair."

When she began to speak, his fingertip pressed gently against her lips. "But it won't work, Joanna. Now it's come down to a choice of being vulnerable or miserable. I need you. I know we're going to have problems, disagreements from time to time—God, we're so different —but it's a risk we'll have to take. Will you marry me? You—"

"Yes."

"—may not feel I even deserve an answer after the way I've behaved, but I hope—" Dark brows lifted in doubt of what he had heard. His voice became husky with longing. "What did you say?"

"I said yes, Simon. I'll marry you. Any other questions?"

"Yes." Her answer seemed to have stunned him. "Where's your bathroom?"

"Down the hall, first door to the left."

He stood, looking down at her. "I'll be right back," he said nervously. "Then we'll talk everything out. We'll make plans. We'll—" A trembling masculine palm went up to rake his hair. "We'll work this out. Don't go away."

"I won't." She watched him walk down the hallway. A man had just asked her to marry him. Not just any man. Simon. The only one that mattered. She'd done everything she could think of to take her mind off him. "Just move that bucket of paint out of your way," she called in afterthought. And now he was here. It was all so magical, so dreamlike. She frowned. Maybe he wasn't in there. Maybe she'd imagined it *this* time too. "Simon," she called, softly at first, then louder. "Simon, are you—still there?"

"Still here," he piped reassuringly.

She sighed. "I love you."

"I love you to-oo."

Joanna closed her eyes with the absolute wonder of hearing him say it. She would make sure they both said it often. When she opened her eyes again, he was standing before her, wiping his fingers with a handkerchief.

"Good paint," he said calmly. "It doesn't come off with soap and water."

"Oil base," she murmured, touched by the patience he showed.

Simon saw the apology in her eyes. He wanted no such thing from her. Only her love. Her tolerance. Putting his handkerchief away, he sat beside her again, glad that her cheek fit so nicely against his chest.

"We're an unlikely pair," he said honestly. "So unlikely that for a long time I couldn't see, didn't *want* to see, any future for us. But you were right all along, Joanna. We have been good for each other. Sometimes I'm a little slow on the uptake, I guess."

"Um." She nodded her complete but delighted agreement.

"There've been times when I wanted to be like you. Others when I wanted you to be like me. Now I realize that none of that is necessary. The only thing I have to do is enjoy you, delight in you, and allow us both to be what we are. God, I've been so stupid." When he heard no response, Simon flashed her a patient glance. "You can interrupt me any time."

She drew back, tilting her chin in a smile. "I wouldn't dream of it, Simon. I want to hear every wonderful word." Joanna rested against him again. "By the way, did I tell you I love you?"

His eyes closed as he sighed, letting the words and their meaning drift slowly inside him. "Yes, you did, but feel free to say it as often as you like. I won't complain."

"You didn't mean it, did you? About losing your nerve?"

"No," he said softly. "I didn't mean it." Just as he was getting used to having her back in his arms, his world, Joanna sat up, a hint of apprehension widening her blue eyes.

"Before we go any further," she whispered, "maybe you'll want to think about something." Her fingers played with the button just above the vee of his sweater. "I'm going to try very hard to make you happy, but—you may not believe this, Simon, but I meant what I said about not being very faithful to housework. As a matter of fact, I hate it."

Keeping the smile at bay, Simon absolutely refused to let his gaze slide anywhere near the clutter on the coffee table. "I see," he said in his most sober voice. "We'll work it out, Joanna."

Her distress disappeared, replaced by the smile he had come to look forward to. He would ask Richard to move, of course, and open up the house for a single family again. A family. His family. And a housekeeper, he added with affection. Simon glanced toward the Christmas tree, shimmering a warm glow through the room. She liked *that* tradition, he mused. Maybe . . .

Unable to keep it to himself any longer, Simon reached inside his pants pocket and drew out the tiny square case. "Joanna, I want you to have this," he said, lifting the lid. "If you'll wear it."

"Oh, Simon." The words were weak when she meant so much more. Joanna stared at the single sapphire, so brilliant that her fingers had begun to ache with anticipation. "Of course, I want to wear it. Why would you think I wouldn't?"

"Well, it's a rather old tradition," he explained, sitting forward to place the ring on her finger. "And you have to admit you're not very—"

She smiled, touched by his concern for her desires, her wishes. "Some traditions are too wonderful to tamper with," she said, holding her hand away to enjoy the sparkling facets of the stone. "My mother will be so thrilled."

He laughed then and the sound was like a soothing, gentle rain to sun-parched earth. "How about you?" he asked. "Are you thrilled?"

"Yes," she whispered. "Oh, yes." Rising to her knees, she let her hands slide around his neck to show him just how deeply thrilled she was. Her kiss was meant to convey all the wonderful feelings she harbored for him. When she asked him to come to her mother's and share Christmas Day, he agreed readily as long as she promised to share the rest of her life with him.

She took him to her bed and there she made love with Simon. It was different for both of them this time. The knowledge of his love invited her to hold nothing back with the man she would cherish for always. The strength of his commitment to her expressed itself most tenderly in the way he kissed her, held her and showed her that loving him would mean more joy than she had ever known before.

Early in the morning while he slept, Joanna wrapped herself in a robe and sat near the window, staring with affection at the ring he had given her. As the first rays of sunlight played over the solitaire, she turned the stone this way and that, watching the facets wink back as though joining her in precious tantalizing conspiracy.

Joanna had never known herself to be overly fond of or careful with jewelry. She had a tendency to lose earrings, one from each pair usually. On her dresser, a tray of singles waited patiently for an unlikely reunion with their mates to prove it. She'd never worn rings much at all. But this one . . . well, she doubted she would ever take off this ring, a sparkling symbol, both public and private, of Simon's love for her. And her sincere return of that love.

"What are you doing?" he asked groggily, lifting himself to sit against the headboard.

"Looking at my ring," she confessed a little smugly.

Joanna slipped out of her robe and got back into bed to cuddle with Simon beneath the covers. In her eagerness, the movement of the water bed tossed them both mercilessly.

"Joanna," he said, fitting his arm around her to draw her close. "I know it's a little soon—we haven't even had the wedding yet—but I'm going to ask you to give up something for me."

"What's that, Simon."

"This bed—except for special occasions of course, like when we want to imagine ourselves making love on the high seas. Or whenever you want for any reason to keep me awake all night."

Joanna smiled, knowing he was exaggerating. She had awakened at least three times during the night, unable to quite believe he was actually here with her. Each time, he'd been sound asleep. Her reassurance had come with the utter joy of holding him, snuggling inside the circle of his arms.

"All right," she said. "I don't mind . . . now that I've got you to rock me with love right down to my toes."

He seemed moved by her admission, his emerald eyes taking on a pseudo-serious expression. "Do I really do that to your toes, Joanna?"

She reached up to kiss his mouth into a smile. "Yes," she replied in a heartfelt whisper. "And so much more. So very much more. Merry Christmas, Simon."

"Um. Same to you, my sweetheart. I know it's going to be the most memorable one I've ever spent."

Joanna would have liked very much to stay there forever with him. But she knew that the world didn't wait for lovers. Not even a novice like her. "If we're going to be on time for my mother's dinner, we'd better get up and get dressed."

But she didn't. She let Simon pull her back to him where she snuggled cozily against his neck. Wrapped in the warmth of his love, she sighed, reminded of a poem Granny had written for her many years before.

"Wouldn't it be nice if we could make time stand still at least for a little while?" she said wistfully.

He smiled, holding her close with tender encouragement. "Go right ahead," he said, his whisper soft and deep. "You've made many moments stand still for me."

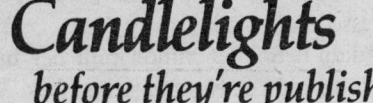

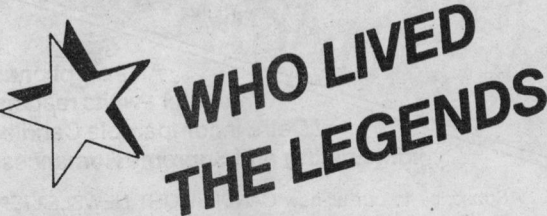